The Last Thing I Remember

Jan Howery

Jan-Carol
Publishing, Inc

"every story needs a book"

The Last Thing I Remember
Whisper Cozy Romance Mystery Series
Jan Howery
Published April 2025
Little Creek Books
Imprint of Jan-Carol Publishing, Inc.
All rights reserved
Copyright © 2025 Jan Howery

ISBN: 978-1-962561-69-3
Library of Congress Control Number: 2025937653

You may contact the publisher:
Jan-Carol Publishing, Inc.
PO Box 701
Johnson City, TN 37605
publisher@jancarolpublishing.com
www.jancarolpublishing.com

My eighth-grade teacher, Ms. Blackwell, had no idea the impact she would have on my life or my future in a writing career when she spoke these simple words to the class after reading my classroom assignment to write a paragraph with three or four sentences describing an event or happening. "This is fantastic! Your punctuation is atrocious, but this writing is just wonderful!" she said.

It is because of her that at the early age of thirteen, I believed that I could write worthy material that people would enjoy reading. I dedicate this and my future writings to her.

Also by Jan Howery

Gone Before Breakfast

Author's Note

Self-published authors and small book presses are sometimes over-looked and overshadowed by the celebrities' books and larger publishers, but these authors and the small publishers are well deserving of a best-selling book. Support local bookstores and local authors by investing in their literary works.

Chapter 1

Samuel Drillenger

Sammie stepped out on the porch of his bungalow in Belize, sat down on the porch swing, and thought, *It's good to feel good again.*

Samuel Drillenger, known as Sammie, grew up in the small rural town of Prestonsburg, Kentucky. After serving four years in the military and being ranked as a marksman-sharpshooter-expert, he graduated from college and medical school. After completing his internship, he returned to Prestonsburg, his hometown, where he built a successful medical practice and career. He became an accomplished and successful surgeon.

Sammie married his high school sweetheart, Melissa, and both were happy to build a life together near family and stay close to their roots. Both attended the same college and married after graduating from college. Melissa was a schoolteacher and loved her work. Sammie's medical practice thrived, and it seemed that he and his wife had the perfect life.

On the night of their 15th wedding anniversary, he and his wife, Melissa, were returning home from a romantic dinner, when a drunk driver ran his truck through a red traffic light at a high rate of speed. The impact hit the passenger's side of their Mercedes Benz car, and as a result Melissa was seriously injured.

Melissa was improving from her injuries when test results found something that Sammie nor Melissa ever suspected. Melissa was diagnosed with stage 4 breast cancer. Treatments and surgeries could not save her life. Six months later, Melissa died.

Sammie struggled for the next two years with guilt, loneliness, and sadness. He decided that he could not continue to practice medicine. He felt that losing his wife and not being able to save her life gave his medical practice no purpose or meaning. Grief directed his daily life and decisions.

Sammie decided to take early retirement, sell his medical practice and his home, leave the area, and just bum around, visiting different resort islands. He traveled to different remote islands, including Belize. After a few months of traveling to the different islands, he was drawn back to Belize and its way of life. He decided to buy an oceanfront bungalow in Corozal situated on Chetumal Bay in northern Belize.

Sammie recognized that Corozal was not a tourist spot and that living there was less expensive than Ambergris Caye. He could drive two hours up Belize's northern highway to the city or drive to Mexico. Corozal was a short 30-minute drive to Chetumal, Mexico, and he could find all the contemporary shopping conveniences. It was perfect for an expat who wanted to live the small-town life but still have "big city" conveniences as an option, and at the same time, enjoy quiet isolation.

When Sammie bought the bungalow, which sat on an acre of land, he was surprised to find a small, old ferryboat out back in the shed. The boat needed a lot of work, but the long hours and many days of refurbishing the boat served as a good therapeutic project for Sammie. When he took the boat out in the water for its first voyage, he was surprised at how comfortable he was as the captain of the boat. The boat glided through the water as he navigated the waves and its engine purred. Sammie felt a freedom that he had never felt before. He knew that living on the water was his life now. He named his boat, *Happiness*.

* * *

It was the day after Christmas when Sammie decided to take the boat out that evening to see the distant fireworks that would continue every night through New Year's Day. It was a beautiful night to just allow the boat to drift while he watched the colorful fireworks light up the sky, alongside the glow of a full moon.

"Perfect night for floating and relaxing on the water," Sammie said to Rufus, his dog. "Let's go."

Rufus, a red-haired mutt, was Sammie's best friend. One late night, Sammie set sail and found the perfect spot to cut off the boat's engine and drift slowly floating on the water. He was relaxing on his boat when he heard a whining sound and spotted movement in the water. He slowly rowed over to the movement and saw a small puppy struggling and fighting to swim and stay alive. Sammie grabbed the puppy and pulled it into the boat. The puppy was so exhausted he collapsed. Sammie nourished him back to health, and since the mutt had red hair and fought for his life like a Roman warrior fighting in battle, he named the dog Rufus. Rufus became Sammie's loyal companion.

Sammie repeated, "Let's go."

Rufus ran and hopped into the boat. Sammie released the ropes from the simple dock and pushed the boat into the water and jumped onto the boat. The water was calm, and the gentle waves glistened by the brightness of the full moon.

Together, they set sail and drifted into the wide bay opening connecting to the ocean waves. It was a perfect spot to watch the fireworks.

When the fireworks ended, the bright glow of the full moon continued to glisten on the water's gentle waves. Sammie lay back, relaxing, and enjoyed the swaying of the boat gently floating in the water.

Sammie closed his eyes. He was falling asleep when the stillness of the night was interrupted by Rufus. Rufus jumped up, leaned over the edge of the boat, and barked loudly.

Sammie, startled, woke up and asked, "What do ya see out there, boy?"

Sammie moved over to the edge of the boat beside Rufus and looked out across the water. "What do you see out there?" Sammie repeated and looked across the waves. "Is there something out there?"

Sammie grabbed his nighttime binoculars from the storage box. He slowly scanned across the calm water. He saw something. "I think... Wait...Holy Being! It's a person!" he said aloud.

The full moon provided light as the boat cut through the gentle waves. Sammie pulled up beside the floating body. *It's a woman, and she's gotta be hurt,* Sammie thought.

He quickly maneuvered the boat closer to her and saw that she was barely hanging onto a life preserver. Her arms appeared to be so weak that she could only drape them over the life preserver and lightly splash the water with her hands. Sammie heard a very faint, low, soft whisper, "Help me."

As Sammie pulled closer to her, he was able to take hold of her shoulders and lift her into the boat. As he lifted her over into his boat, he heard a very faint, low, soft whisper again, "Please help me."

Rufus continued to bark loudly and jumped around and around.

"Rufus, sit and stay," Sammie commanded. "We have an injured lady here and she needs our help."

Rufus immediately obeyed.

"It'll be okay," Sammie said reassuringly to the woman, even though he had doubts of her survival. The woman's body was covered in blood. Blood oozed from a large gash on her head. It was not the only wound on her head. She had another cut on the back of her head, one cut above her eye, and bruises on her face and on her body. Her clothes were torn and in shreds on her small frame.

"We gotta get her some help," Sammie said as he revved up the boat and sped toward his bungalow.

Chapter 2

The night air was warm with a light breeze. Sammie quickly maneuvered his boat to his small dock. Rufus jumped out of the boat and ran to the front porch. The woman was unconscious. Sammie knew that she was barely hanging on to life. He picked up the woman and carried her like a sack of potatoes thrown across his back.

"You're sure a light load," Sammie said as he carried her up the steps to the porch and slowly opened the front door. He placed her body on the sofa and looked at her. Rufus followed him inside and lay down and watched.

Sammie examined the woman's head and looked at her wet clothes barely draped on her body. "We gotta get her out of these wet clothes and examine for other injuries," he said out loud.

Sammie walked into his bedroom, opened his closet, grabbed a shirt, and looked for a pair of tight-fitting jogging pants. "Yup, these are too small for me. Perfect," he said. He then pushed all the clothes in the closet to one side, and in the back of his closet was his private safe, hidden behind a fake door.

Sammie decided a safe was needed for the protection of his personal papers, guns, bullets, and cash. He also had a large supply of prescription medicines and medical supplies, as well as a huge gun selection, with an arsenal stored in the room-sized safe.

"Once an M.D., always an M.D.," Sammie said and snickered as he grabbed his medical bag. From the bedroom, he grabbed a blanket, and from the bathroom he grabbed towels and hair clippers. He walked back to the living room and looked at the woman lying on the sofa. *Her injuries are so bad and she's still bleeding,* he thought. He sat down on the sofa next to her and brushed her hair back from the head wound.

"You need sutures…lots of 'em," Sammie said. "I hate to do this, but I'm gonna shave your head."

Sammie pulled her hair back into a towel, covered the wound with a loose bandage, and ripped her water-soaked torn blouse. It fell to the floor. He admired her breasts and thought, *Keep it professional.* He tore her pants along the seam and slowly removed them, as well as her panties. Sammie dried her body with towels and slowly put his jogging pants on her naked body. He saw many bruises over her body. He covered her breasts with a towel and removed the towel wrapped around her hair. He proceeded to shave her head. The woman moaned, and she tried to wave her arms in the air.

"Easy…easy…it's gonna be alright," Sammie said and tried to reassure her. After he finished shaving her head, he walked to the kitchen, got a glass of water, and a couple of pain pills out of his medical bag. He walked over to her, lifted her head, and placed the pills in her mouth. She slowly sipped the water and swallowed the pills.

"Good girl, and that'll help keep you relaxed," Sammie said.

Sammie washed the wound with soap and water and hydrogen peroxide. He also applied an anesthetic to the head wound. He took the special needle and thread and began to stitch on the head wound slowly and meticulously.

"Finally…23 sutures with a few over there and a couple over here," Sammie said. "But you've lost a lot of blood. You need to go the hospital."

By now it was early morning. The woman remained unconscious and didn't move. Sammie changed his clothes and put on a clean shirt and pants. He put one of his shirts on the woman and wrapped her in a blanket. He gathered her up, carrying her and placing her in the back of his older Honda SUV.

"Rufus, boy, you stay here and watch things," Sammie yelled out the window as he pulled out of the driveway and headed to the Corozal Community Hospital.

* * *

Sammie was very familiar with the Corozal Community Hospital. He worked there as a volunteer. Everyone knew him as Dr. Sammie and appreciated the time that he donated to the hospital. He volunteered every third weekend and if the hospital was shorthanded, the on-call personnel would reach out to him. The doctors and staff respected his knowledge and experience.

On his way to the hospital, Sammie used his cell phone and called the hospital. "Corozal Community Hospital. How may I help you?"

Hey, is this Maria?" Sammie asked.

"Yes, how may I help you?" she asked.

"This is Dr. Sammie. Meet me at the emergency entrance with a stretcher. I have an injured woman who appears to have been in a boating accident," Sammie instructed.

"Oh my! Yes, I'll see that there is someone waiting for you when you arrive. Are you close?" Maria asked.

"I should be there in about 20 minutes," Sammie said. "Who's working emergency today?"

"Dr. Sanchez is on duty," Maria answered.

"Good. I'll be there shortly. Thanks." Sammie ended the phone call.

Chapter 3

Sammie drove quickly and arrived at the hospital in the predicted 20 minutes. As he pulled up to the emergency entrance, the doors opened and two nurses with a stretcher motioned for him to pull his vehicle closer to the emergency entrance.

He followed their guidance, parked, jumped out, and opened the side door of the SUV. Together they lifted the woman's body and placed her on the stretcher. The nurses rushed the woman inside and Sammie got back in his SUV and parked it and rushed inside the hospital.

A nurse was waiting for Sammie when he entered. "She's in examining room four."

"Thank you," Sammie said as he rushed by the nurse.

Sammie walked inside the examination room and was greeted by Dr. Sanchez. "Are you scouting out patients for us?" Dr. Sanchez asked and smiled.

Sammie smiled and answered, "Looks that way."

"This lady is pretty beat up. I see the very meticulously placed sutures. I assumed you did them. So, what happened here?" Dr. Sanchez asked seriously.

"Late last night, I found her floating in the bay. I rushed her home, and that head wound was bleeding pretty badly. I felt it was necessary to have immediate attention," Sammie answered.

"Yes, Dr. Sammie, you're right. She's probably lost a lot of blood, and we are getting a blood supply for her. Those cuts are deep. We'll do some tests, X-rays, and of course, a CT scan. Let's hope there's no intracranial hematoma. Did you do a complete exam?" Dr. Sanchez asked.

"I don't think there are any broken bones, but she has a lot of bruising. When I found her floating in the water, she was hanging onto a life preserver. I did give her five milligrams of Diazepam before the sutures. She was combative and needed to be still," Sammie explained.

"How long ago?" Dr. Sanchez asked.

"Three hours or so," Sammie said. "Do you know if anyone has filed a missing persons report?"

"I'm not sure," Dr. Sanchez said. He turned to the nurse in the room and asked, "Has there been any missing persons report?"

"Not locally. We had a report earlier to come in that a woman from the USA had not shown up at the airport in Mexico, and her family reported her missing," the nurse replied.

"Mexico?" Sammie asked.

"It was reported that she was an ex-girlfriend of a well-known drug lord. She was visiting family in Chetumal, Mexico. And when she didn't show up at the airport to return to Florida, her family reported her missing," the nurse said.

"When did this report come in?" Sammie asked.

"Around midnight," the nurse answered.

Sammie looked at the woman lying there and barely hanging onto life, and thought, *She doesn't seem to fit an image of a person who would do illegal drugs.*

"I don't think she fits the description," the nurse said, interrupting Sammie's thoughts.

"We need to get started ASAP on her care," Dr. Sanchez instructed.

"Yes," Sammie said. "I'll be in the employee's lounge. I think that I'll hang around here for a while if you need anything."

"Perfect," Dr. Sanchez said.

Sammie walked down the long hallway to the employee lounge. The lounge had several large sofas where hospital personnel would take breaks, rest, and take naps. It was a very large room with a kitchen, tables, vending machines, and three large coffee pots. Many employees would bring food and place it on the table and in the refrigerator.

Sammie walked over to the coffee pot, grabbed a coffee cup from the cabinet, and poured himself a cup of coffee. He helped himself to a piece of cake on the table and sat down at the table. Laying on the table was a local newspaper. He opened the newspaper, searching for the sports section. He read through the sports section and started to put the newspaper pages back in order when he noticed a full page of pictures. At the top of the page, the words were:

Resort Celebrates the Holiday Season with Locals and Tourists!

Below the header, were lots of photos of people, children, and activities. Sammie looked at the photos when one of them caught his attention. He stared at it and took a closer look at the photo. *That's her!* he thought. He looked closer. There were a couple of women with her in the picture. *It really does look like her*, he thought. Below the photo, the caption was:

Tour groups enjoy the fun activities!

Sammie was startled when a nurse walked into the lounge and said, "Dr. Sammie, Dr. Sanchez would like to speak with you."

"Sure. Thank you, I'll be right there." Sammie ripped the photo out of the newspaper and put it in his shirt pocket.

Sammie walked back to the examining room to find the nurses preparing the woman for admittance to a patient's room. Dr. Sanchez walked in and said, "We're going to keep her for a while. The scan has not been read yet, but it appears that she doesn't have any broken bones. We don't have any ID for her. Protocol requires us to notify police since she has no ID."

"Let's wait and see what happens. When she wakes, she'll be able to give us details," Sammie said assuredly. "And I'll stick around and keep watch on her."

"Well . . . okay. We'll see, but that is a nasty bump on the head," Dr. Sanchez said.

* * *

Sammie stayed at the hospital day and night, only going home to shower, change clothes, check on things, and feed Rufus. It was now four days since Sammie found the woman floating in the water, and it was New Year's Eve. The woman patient had only stirred a little and was still comatose and unresponsive.

Sammie was sitting in her room when Dr. Sanchez walked in. "Our patient is slow to come around," Dr. Sanchez said. "Her vitals are good, and there's been eye movement, and she seems to be improving. There's brain activity, and her neurological reflexes are affirmative. So, it is up to her, but I do believe she will come around."

"The head injury and the shock were traumatic for her," Sammie said. "But I think that she'll come around soon, too."

"I'm going to be celebrating the New Year at a party with friends this evening. Would you like to join us?" Dr. Sanchez asked Sammie.

"Thank you. No. I'm going to stay here. I'll head home to change, but I know that there'll be a light crew here tonight, so I'll come back and hang around here to help out if needed," Sammie said.

"Much appreciated," Dr. Sanchez said. "And Happy New Year."

"Happy New Year to you," Sammie said as Dr. Sanchez exited the room.

Sammie looked at the unconscious woman lying motionlessly in the hospital bed. "You are a beautiful woman. You are going to wake, and you're going to celebrate the New Year," Sammie said with prediction and smiled.

Chapter 4

Sammie rushed home around 6:00 p.m. He showered, fed Rufus, and hurried back to the hospital. As Sammie walked through the front doors of the hospital, Sammie heard fireworks from a distance. *I guess the New Year's celebrations have already started*, Sammie thought.

Sammie entered the woman's room, and the woman's body suddenly jerked as if she had been startled. She awoke and looked around the room. She looked at Sammie very wide-eyed.

"Well, hello," Sammie said friendly. "How are you feeling?"

The woman slowly moved, sat up, and reached for her head.

"No, don't touch your bandages. You had a nasty boating accident, and you have wounds on your head," Sammie said calmly and walked over, positioning her pillow behind her.

She lowered her hand and looked at Sammie. "I hurt," she whispered. "My head hurts."

"I'm sure. Are you thirsty? Would you like something to eat or drink?" Sammie asked.

"Water," she whispered.

Sammie walked over to the table next to her bed, poured a cup of water, and handed it to her. She took a sip. She had a frightened facial expression on her face, and she looked all around the room as if confused.

"Where am I?" she asked and took another sip of water.

"You're at the Corozal Community Hospital," Sammie said slowly.

"Where?" she asked, puzzled.

"Corozal Community Hospital...near Belize," Sammie said and watched her very closely.

"Belize? Hospital?" she asked. "How...why...what happened?"

"It appears that you were in a boating accident. I was out in my boat and found you...floating in the water," Sammie said cautiously.

The woman looked at Sammie and around the room again. Nothing seemed familiar to her.

"My name is Sammie," Sammie said. "What's your name?"

"My name is..." She stopped. "My name is...I...I don't think I remember...I can't remember my name!" she said in a panic. "I don't remember, and I don't remember my name. I don't understand. I don't know who you are or where I am, or how I got here. I don't remember my name!" she screamed, becoming highly agitated.

The nurses heard her yell and rushed into her room. "It's okay," Sammie said. "It's a normal reaction."

The woman began to tremble and shake.

"Calm down," Sammie said sternly. "Calm down and take deep breaths. Now...breathe with me...in...and out...in and out...continue ...breathe with me. Focus on me. On me...breathe...in and out..."

This continued for a few minutes, and the woman slowly calmed down. Sammie told the nurses that everything was okay and he would stay with her. He instructed them to bring her light food to eat.

Still, in a panic-stricken mode, she stared at Sammie.

Sammie asked firmly, "Now...tell me...what is the last thing that you do remember?"

The woman stared at Sammie as if she were in deep thought.

"What is the last thing you remember?" Sammie repeated.

The woman took a deep breath and answered, "I remember that I was in the water, and I was so scared. I was so scared," she said, and tears swelled in her eyes. "I was in the water...and someone pulled me into a boat…and being pulled into the boat…is…the last thing I remember."

"That's good," Sammie said. "You do remember things. And with that head wound, it is important that you can remember some things."

The look on her face was total concentration. "I was in the water… and I was so scared. I was so scared…I thought I was going to die," she said as tears streamed down her face.

"Do you remember how you ended up in the water?" Sammie asked.

The woman went back into a thoughtful trance. She shook her head no.

"Okay. No more questions. I want you to rest," Sammie said. "Rest is very important."

The nurse entered her room with a soft diet dinner. "I hope that this is okay, Dr. Sammie. I brought soup, pudding, and orange juice," the nurse said and set the tray down on the bedside table.

"Yes. Perfect," Sammie said and smiled as the nurse walked out of the room.

Boom! Boom! Boom!

"What's that?" the woman patient asked frantically.

"It's New Year's Eve," Sammie answered. "You're hearing fireworks for the New Year's celebration."

"New Year's Eve?" the woman asked slowly. "What…"

She was interrupted by Sammie, "I want you to try to eat at least a few bites and then rest."

"She called you, Dr. Sammie. Are you my doctor?" the woman asked hesitantly.

"Yes, I am a doctor, but I'm retired. I work here as a volunteer as they need me," Sammie said and smiled. "So, doctor's orders…eat and rest and try not to worry. With your type of head injuries, to have post-traumatic amnesia or dissociative amnesia is to be expected."

"Amnesia? Amnesia? So, when will my memory come back?" the woman asked anxiously. "I don't remember my name."

"Give it time. Just try to relax and give it time," Sammie replied. "But, for now, you need a name. I'm going to call you ...Sunshine."

"Sunshine?" the woman asked. "Why Sunshine?"

"Because ...tomorrow, the sun is going to shine, and you will too," Sammie said and smiled.

The woman smiled a weak smile and took a sip of the soup.

Chapter 5

It was six days into the new year, and Dr. Sanchez was making his rounds at the hospital. He walked into Sunshine's room and saw Dr. Sammie sitting and talking to Sunshine.

"How's our patient doing today?" Dr. Sanchez said and smiled.

"She will start her physical therapy soon, and her wounds are healing nicely, so, I think it's time that she be relocated to another place to continue on her path of healing," Dr. Sammie said. "I would like to discuss that with you, Dr. Sanchez."

"Sure. I agree. Meet me in my office," Dr. Sanchez suggested.

"No. You discuss it in front of me. Where am I going to go?" Sunshine demanded to know.

"Okay. Here it is. I suggest that you come and live with me, and I'll be sure that you get to your physical therapy appointments as well as your therapist appointments. Being out of this hospital environment here will do you good in getting your memory back online. Would you consider that?" Dr. Sammie asked joyfully.

"That can't be a choice," Dr. Sanchez said firmly. "We were supposed to report her to the authorities, and we didn't. We must report this because we're responsible for her care. The only choice is to move her to the mental health rehab wing."

"The Psych Ward? With the mental patients?" Sunshine asked with surprise. "No, I won't go. I'm not crazy."

"I am sorry, but you can't stay here. Your care doesn't require our services as a patient," Dr. Sanchez said. "I think that if you stay in the mental health rehab wing, you'll continue to improve."

"Wait…just wait a minute. I can take her. I'll be responsible for her well-being, her bills, and everything. She'll not fit in with the other patients. You know that. It'll do more harm than good," Dr. Sammie said sternly.

"Why would you do that?" Sunshine asked. "You don't know me… or do you?"

"No, I don't know you, and we had never met until the night I pulled you out of the water. But I do know that I brought you here to the hospital and you were in my care. If you'll just trust me, I promise you'll continue to get good care," Dr. Sammie said.

"In exchange for what?" Sunshine asked bitterly.

"Absolutely nothing," Dr. Sammie said firmly. "No strings attached. I just want you to get the best care, because I'm sure you'll completely recover soon."

"You can't know that, Dr. Sammie. And what about the authorities?" Dr. Sanchez said.

"I'll take responsibility for that, too," Dr. Sammie assured him.

Dr. Sanchez looked at Sunshine and said, "I guess it's up to you."

"I don't guess I have a choice. I certainly don't want to be locked up in a mental health ward," Sunshine said sadly.

"I promise you'll have good care, and once you get out of here, things might look familiar to you. You'll have a better opportunity to improve mentally," Dr. Sammie said. "And as a retired doctor, I am qualified to care for you."

"But you're a stranger to me," Sunshine said shyly.

"Isn't everyone?" Dr. Sammie asked and smiled and winked. "You're more acquainted with me than anyone."

Sunshine nodded affirmatively.

"Sunshine, you can call me anytime if you feel uncomfortable," Dr. Sanchez said. "I'll give you my cell number and you can call me anytime."

"Yes. That's a good idea. That way, if you're uncomfortable, you'll have someone you can contact," Dr. Sammie said and nodded at Dr. Sanchez.

Sunshine looked down at the hospital gown that she was wearing and asked, "Where are my clothes?"

"I bought some clothes for you, and they're in the closet there. I hope they fit. So, get dressed and we'll get started on your journey of complete recovery," Sammie said.

Sunshine looked at Dr. Sammie and then at Dr. Sanchez.

"Okay, but Dr. Sanchez, I do want your phone number," Sunshine said reluctantly.

Chapter 6

It had been almost six weeks since Sammie found Sunshine floating in the bay and pulled her out of the water. Her head injuries were healing nicely, but her memory had not returned. Sunshine adjusted to living at Sammie's house. She had privacy with her own bedroom and bath and felt more comfortable with each passing day.

During the six weeks, Sammie drove Sunshine to her physical therapy three times a week and to her psychological visits every other day. He shared personal experiences and his life stories about his career and deceased wife, hoping that it would trigger her memories. Sunshine enjoyed listening to his stories.

Other than going to her doctor's appointments, Sunshine was uncomfortable going out in public or out to dinner, so Sammie always got food to-go or cooked meals for them. It was a beautiful evening when Sammie decided to cook hamburgers on the grill. Sunshine walked out on the deck carrying utensils and hamburger buns and said, "Those burgers smell delicious."

"My special recipe," Sammie said and smiled. "But aren't you tired of my cooking?"

"Nope. You're a good cook," Sunshine said and grinned. "You've spoiled me with you doing all the cooking."

"Well, I think it's time that we go out to dinner. Get you back out around people, places, and since Friday is Valentine's Day…I've made dinner reservations for us at that fancy resort. I thought it might do you good to have a change of scenery," Sammie said and didn't look at Sunshine.

"I don't think that I can go out...with no hair," Sunshine said sadly.

"I know that you always wear a hooded sweatshirt, but how about we go shopping and you can get a scarf or something? Will that make you feel better? You can buy some clothes and anything else you might need," Sammie said sweetly.

"I owe you so much, Sammie. I have no money and no memory if I do or don't have any money or means of support. How can you afford to do all this for me? I owe you so much," Sunshine said apologetically.

"Don't worry about money. All is good. I've got it taken care of," Sammie said and winked. "And besides, just going to therapy and visiting your psychologist is not giving you a chance to meet other people. Getting out and seeing other people and having different scenery may be good therapy for you."

"Are you getting tired of my company?" Sunshine asked and smiled.

"Of course not," Sammie said. "Rufus and I enjoy your company. Don't we, boy?"

Rufus wagged his tail as if to agree.

"But it'll do us both good. Besides, I think that you know that you probably don't live here and you're not a local, which means you were visiting...or you were on vacation. So, how did you end up in the water? I just think it's time for you to see places, people, and things...Maybe something will feel familiar to you. Are you up for it?" Sammie asked seriously.

Sunshine hesitated. *Maybe I should,* she thought. She reluctantly said, "I guess so."

* * *

The next day, after Sunshine's psychology visit, Sammie and Sunshine went shopping. They stopped at a couple of ladies' shops. Sunshine enjoyed looking at clothes and trying on different outfits.

They stopped at an upscale boutique, and the owner approached. "Are you looking for something special today?" she asked.

Sunshine hesitated and said sheepishly, "I need…a scarf…or something to cover my head. Recommendations?"

"Oh honey," the owner said, "I can fix you up with a matching outfit with a pre-tied head scarf with pretty colors to coordinate with your outfit. Follow me. And my name is Editha."

Sunshine looked at Sammie, and he said, "Go ahead. I'll go find me a cup of coffee down the street. I'll be back in an hour or so."

The shop had a light fresh lavender fragrance and a sophisticated fresh look. The boutique owner, Editha, led Sunshine to a backroom with rows of pre-tied head scarves. "I work with cancer patients, and I understand what you're looking for. Are your scars from cancer? I mean, your head was shaved," she asked with concern.

"No, no cancer. I was in a boating accident, and the wounds had to be stitched, and my head was shaved. The scars are still visible," Sunshine said, changing the subject. "You do have a large collection here."

"What are your favorite colors?" Editha asked enthusiastically.

Sunshine stared blankly. *I don't remember what my favorite colors are*, she thought.

Editha observed Sunshine's hesitation and said, "You don't know. That's okay. Are you going out to somewhere special?"

Sunshine quickly answered, "Yes. We have Valentine's Day dinner plans at the nearby resort."

"Oh…well…I hear that the resort is uptown. For Valentine's Day, let's get you in something with red and white," Editha said.

Sunshine tried on different outfits and decided on a few tops and shorts. For dinner, Sunshine decided on a white pair of slacks with a red, off-the-shoulder, loose-flowing blouse. The head scarf was colorful with an array of colors of red, white, and rose design.

"This outfit is perfect on you," Editha said and positioned the headscarf on Sunshine's head.

Sunshine stared in the mirror. Her eyes were fixed on her white slacks. *White slacks*, she thought. *They seem familiar.*

Her thoughts were interrupted when Editha said, "You are so beautiful. Your man won't be flirting with no other woman. That's for sure."

"Flirting…flirting…" Sunshine said and repeated the words quietly. *Why does that sound familiar?* she thought.

The frown on Sunshine caused Editha to think that she might have said something that offended Sunshine. "I'm sorry. I was just kidding. I know that your man isn't no flirt," Editha said and tried to backtrack her comment in her best broken English.

"Oh…I'm sorry. You didn't say anything wrong. I was just lost in my thoughts. And I'm afraid I'm getting a headache, and I'm finding it hard to concentrate," Sunshine said. "Just having too much fun here."

They both laughed out loud.

"What's so funny?" a voice echoed from the front of the shop.

"That's your man," Editha said and walked out of the dressing room to the front of the shop. "Your special lady got the perfect outfit, and you won't be disappointed."

"Perfect. And thank you," Sammie said and winked.

Sunshine changed and carried the clothes to the counter, and Sammie paid for the purchases.

"Thank you both! And Happy Valentine's Day…early," Editha said with a smile as she handed purchases to Sunshine.

Sammie and Sunshine stopped by a pharmacy, and Sunshine purchased makeup and personal items. It was a full day of shopping, and they arrived home in the late afternoon. When Sammie drove into the driveway, he broke the silence and said, "You're sort of quiet. You feel okay?"

"Yes," Sunshine answered with a smile. She paused and asked, "Sammie, what was I wearing when you found me? I mean, what kind of clothes did I have on?"

Sammie was surprised at the question. He hesitated and replied, "Your clothes were pretty torn, and messed up. Your blouse was mostly in shreds. But you were wearing white pants, but they were also dirty and torn and bloody. There was a lot of blood. The clothes you had on were tossed away. Why do you ask?"

"Was just curious. Today, I didn't remember my favorite color when Editha asked, but when I tried on the white pants, they seemed familiar to me," Sunshine shared.

"That's good," Sammie said. "Little bits and pieces of reminders are good indicators that your memory will come back. So, are you okay?"

"Yes, just tired," Sunshine said.

"Well, I'll fix us something to eat, and you rest up then. You and I have got big plans for tomorrow evening," Sammie said and winked.

Chapter 7

The next day went by quickly, and Sunshine was excited to get dressed for dinner. *I am going out to dinner*, she thought. *Wonder if I did this often? It seems to make me happy to be going to dinner*, she thought, and at the same time, she felt confused.

"Are you ready?" Sammie yelled from the door and stood on the front porch.

"Coming," Sunshine answered. She took one last look in the mirror and thought, *I've done this before.*

Sunshine walked to the doorway and Sammie turned and saw her standing there. "Wow! Just look at you. You are stunning," Sammie said with a twinkle in his eye.

"Thank you! You are so kind," Sunshine said and smiled. Then she became very serious. "Are you sure this is a good idea?" she asked.

"Sure do," Sammie said. "Come on. Our taxi is waiting."

"Taxi? We have a taxi?" Sunshine asked.

"Yes. The resort offers water taxi services to nearby islands. And we are so close, I thought it would be nice to be escorted to the resort," Sammie said.

"You do think of everything," Sunshine said and walked past him to the dock.

"Watch your step," Sammie said.

"Yes. I don't think that I want to go swimming anytime soon," Sunshine said with a snicker.

The ride on the water taxi was smooth, and soon Sammie and Sunshine were at the resort's dock.

"Look at all the yachts. Look at them," Sunshine said in astonishment. "There are some really large yachts here."

"Yup. Some expensive boats," Sammie said in agreement.

"Oh, look. That yacht…its name is *Gone*…" Sunshine said but was interrupted.

"Sunshine!" Sammie yelled. "Watch your step!"

Sunshine quickly looked around and realized that she was about to miss a step. "Thank you! I should be watching where I'm going!"

Sammie took ahold of her arm and they both stepped onto the long dock. They were greeted by the resort's transportation driver on a modified golf cart. Sammie turned and paid the water taxi driver. "Will you be available later?" Sammie asked the driver.

"Yes, sir. Just request it when you are ready to leave. Thank you, sir," the water taxi driver said and pulled away from the dock.

Sammie turned to the cart driver, and asked, "Are you our escort to the restaurant?"

"Yes, sir! And welcome. Is this your first visit or are you returning?" he asked.

"This is our first visit, and we're so excited to see this beautiful resort. We've heard such wonderful things about the resort," Sammie said.

"Well, let me give you a quick presentation," the driver said. "The resort was a vision of two brothers and is named *My Beautiful Lady*. Over to the right is the small hotel for guests…about 75 rooms. Across here, at the marina, are 40 one- and two-bedroom huts for guests. And what you see on the hilltop there…That is the main house and hotel. The owners live here on the very top floor. And there are three floors with conference rooms and dining rooms on the bottom floor. All with an ocean view!"

"It's a Grand Hacienda and just…" Sunshine said, stopping mid-sentence.

Sammie looked at Sunshine and asked, "Are you okay? Is there something familiar?"

Sunshine hesitated and sighed, "No…No, there's nothing familiar."

The driver arrived at the hotel front entrance. Sammie and Sunshine were greeted by a smiling guide. "Welcome! Are you here for dinner?" he asked.

"Yes," Sammie said. "We're early. Our reservations are set for seven."

"No problem. Let me guide you to the restaurant and to the outdoor balcony where you can watch the sunset, have a drink, and enjoy the views, and we'll call you for dinner," the guide said and led them to the restaurant.

The hostess at the restaurant greeted them. "Hi, welcome to Sunset View restaurant."

"Thank you," Sammie said to the guide and turned to the restaurant hostess. "We have dinner reservations at seven."

"Great, and I hope you arrived early to see that beautiful sunset," the hostess said, friendly.

"Yes, we did," Sammie replied.

"Perfect and follow me. Is this your first time visiting?" the hostess asked.

"Yes, it is," Sammie said.

"Wonderful. Thank you for joining us this evening. We have a special Valentine's evening planned with entertaining music and special dishes prepared just for Valentine's Day. You may sit on our private oceanfront bar, on the balcony, offering complimentary appetizers served on the balcony, and enjoy the sunset. We'll call you for your dinner seating," the hostess said and guided them to the balcony.

"This is exquisite," Sunshine said and smiled, staring out at the ocean. "Look at this view."

"Would you like a high-top table?" the hostess asked. "Or sit on the sofa?"

"High-top would be nice," Sunshine quickly replied.

"No problem, and all have wonderful sunset views," the hostess said and directed them to the high-top table. "Your server will be with you shortly with our appetizer menu, all complimentary. Enjoy your evening. We'll escort you to your table at your dinner reservation time."

Sammie and Sunshine enjoyed non-alcoholic drinks and appreciated the spectacular views. At approximately seven o'clock, the hostess directed Sammie and Sunshine to their table for dinner.

Chapter 8

Lisa, the Travel Director, and the sister of the two brothers who own the resort, sat at the bar waiting for Allison, her future sister-in-law, to join her. She ordered two vodka and soda drinks. As the drinks were served, Allison walked up to the bar.

"Hey, I thought we were meeting the guys at the yacht," Allison said and sat down and took a sip of her drink.

"Well, I thought so, too. But at the last minute, my wonderful husband told me that we would meet here in the bar," Lisa said sarcastically.

"Todd told you that?" Allison asked.

"Yes. What did Buckie tell you?" Lisa asked.

"Well…your wonderful brother told me to talk to you," Allison said and laughed.

Lisa giggled.

"There's a lot of people coming in for dinner reservations," Allison said and looked around the room.

"Valentine's Day is pretty popular," Lisa said. "Most are guests, but some are locals."

Lisa looked at Allison, who seemed to be lost in thought. "What's on your mind?" Lisa asked.

"I was just thinking how Valentine's Day has always been full of surprises for me…in the past," Allison said seriously. "From happiness to sadness."

"Yeah. Does seem so. And I know that you must think about Jan, too," Lisa said and took a sip of her cocktail.

"I miss her so much. She and I were so excited when we celebrated Valentine's Day in St. Thomas with..." Allison said but was interrupted.

"...with Buckie and Winston," Lisa said and winked. "Let's hope that this Valentine's Day is full of happiness."

"It is! I've never been happier," Allison said excitedly and glanced down at her watch. "I think I'll visit the ladies' room before we leave. The guys will be here any minute."

Lisa smiled and nodded.

* * *

Allison walked out of the bar area, turned right, and walked down the long hallway to the ladies' room. She pushed open the door, looked in the mirror, and decided she needed to freshen her lipstick. She took out her lipstick case from her purse, freshened her lips, and started to place her lipstick case back into her purse, when the ladies' room door opened. She casually glanced over to the woman who entered. Allison was so startled when she saw the woman, she gasped. She stared. She couldn't move. She just looked at the woman with a frozen stare.

"I'm sorry I startled you," Sunshine said and smiled. Sunshine stared back at Allison. There was a moment of silence, and they both looked at each other. Sunshine, puzzled, broke the silence and asked, "Do...have...have we met before?"

The question caught Allison off guard. She dropped her purse and lipstick case, both hitting the floor.

"Oh no. Let me help you," Sunshine said graciously.

"No!" Allison said and quickly grabbed her purse and lipstick case from the floor and stumbled past Sunshine. Allison pushed the door open and rushed out.

"I am sorry," Sunshine said again as Allison rushed out the door.

Allison struggled to breathe and rushed down the hallway. She felt numb. *That was Jan! Heaven above! That was Jan! She's dead, but that was Jan.* Her thoughts were racing.

Allison collapsed on the bar stool next to Lisa and grabbed her cocktail and swallowed a big gulp.

"What the hell happened to you in the bathroom? You look like you just saw a ghost," Lisa said, staring at Allison.

Allison hesitated. She looked at Lisa and slowly said, "I did."

"You did what?" Lisa asked.

"I just saw a ghost," Allison said, staring at the cocktail.

"You saw a ghost," Lisa said and giggled. "You must have. You sure do look like it. You're trembling."

"I…I just saw…Jan…in the bathroom," Allison murmured.

"What did you say?" Lisa asked.

Allison looked at Lisa and choked out her words, "I saw Jan. It was her. She had a turban on, and I could see scars on her face and head, but it was Jan. I tell you…it was Jan."

"Okay. Get a grip. We were just talking about her, and you just saw her. Your mind is just overloaded. Just breathe. You know that Jan is dead," Lisa calmly said.

"No. She's alive," Allison said, confused and puzzled.

"Allison, you're scaring me. Jan is dead. You took her urn to Virginia and had her service," Lisa said sternly.

"She didn't recognize me. She spoke to me and even wanted to know if we knew each other. I know…it was her," Allison insisted, ignoring Lisa's comments.

"The ghost talked to you," Lisa said sarcastically.

"She's not a ghost. She's real and she's alive. You'll see. She'll come out…Look…There she is!" Allison said and nodded her head in the woman's direction. She looked back at Lisa. "There…walking to that far back table."

Lisa slowly turned and watched the woman walk to the table.

"I see the woman wearing a turban, but I don't see her face," Lisa said while appearing to be looking around the room.

"It's her. I tell you, it is Jan," Allison repeated.

"Winston identified the body. You buried her. Jan is dead," Lisa insisted.

"No. You have to see for yourself. It's Jan," Allison said and took another drink.

"Okay. I'll find out," Lisa said. She took out business cards from her purse. "I'll slowly make my way over to their table. Watch me."

Lisa walked to two different tables and introduced herself as the resort's Travel Director, and she was available to secure excursions or tours for their vacation experience.

Lisa made her way to the table where the woman was seated. She looked and greeted Sammie and handed a business card to him and said, "Hi. Welcome. I am the resort's Travel Director, Lisa, and if you would like…" Lisa stopped in mid-sentence as she glanced over to the woman. She gasped and stared. *It is Jan,* she thought.

"Are you okay?" Sammie asked.

Trying to compose herself, Lisa answered, "Uh…uh…oh yes."

"This is my friend, Sunshine," Sammie said. "We have never visited this fine resort before, but we have heard wonderful things about it."

Lisa looked back at Sammie, "I…I can assist you with a tour if you would like. We offer excursions and we can accommodate events and family reunions."

Lisa glanced back to Sunshine and said, "Sunshine is an interesting name. You…I…you remind me of someone I used to know."

Sammie interrupted and didn't give Sunshine a chance to reply. "Yes. I'll keep your card, and we may look to set a time for a tour," Sammie said.

The conversation was interrupted when the server walked up with the drink and dinner menus.

Lisa looked back at Sammie and said, "Yes, of course. Please feel free to call me. I hope you enjoy your dinner."

"Thank you, and it was a pleasure meeting you," Sammie said.

"My pleasure," Lisa said and turned and walked away.

She made her way back to her bar stool, and she, too, collapsed on the stool. "We both just saw a real ghost," Lisa said and took a big sip of her drink. "That is Jan."

"I told you. But how can that be? She didn't recognize me. She doesn't seem to know us," Allison said. "But it is her."

"She is supposed to be dead," Lisa said. "Winston identified the body."

"Well, she isn't dead. And she doesn't know who we are," Allison said. "I think I'll go over there and find out what's going on. Winston was supposed to have identified the body. So, who did he identify? Who did I carry to Virginia? It wasn't Jan."

"Look at her," Lisa said. "She's wearing a turban. She has no hair. She's got a nasty scar on the side of her head. I bet her head was shaved due to a head injury. Maybe … maybe with that head injury, she can't remember things."

"Amnesia?" Allison asked, puzzled. "You think that she has amnesia?"

"Yes. Didn't she ask you if you knew her?" Lisa said.

"Yes. So, she can't remember that we were best friends. I don't understand," Allison said. "But I guess that could explain it. But it doesn't explain how she is alive, and not dead. How did Winston identify the wrong person?"

At that moment, Lisa's cell phone jiggled with a text message.

Where are you ladies? We are on the yacht. Waiting.

"It's Todd. They're on the yacht waiting for us," Lisa said. "We gotta go."

Lisa texted back. **Both on way.**

"So, what are we going to do?" Allison asked.

"Nothing. Don't mention it. We're going to wait until I can figure out what to do, but in the meantime…" Lisa said as she took her cell phone and strategically took photos of the dining room as if to take photos of the guests enjoying their dining experience. "Got it," she said and dropped her phone in her purse. "We now have proof. Jan is alive. Let's go. We can't keep our men waiting. Aren't they in for a surprise?" Lisa said and smiled with a twinkle in her eye.

"So, are we going to tell them?" Allison asked as they walked out of the bar.

"Oh no. Not yet," Lisa said firmly.

Lisa and Allison were escorted on a cart down to the dock, and saw Todd and Buckie, standing on the yacht.

"Where have you been?" Todd asked impatiently as Lisa and Allison stepped onto the yacht.

"You told me that you were going to meet us in the bar," Lisa snapped.

When Lisa and Allison stepped on the yacht, they immediately saw two tables set for dining with champagne, appetizers, and a dozen red roses on each table.

"Oh my! You and Buckie did this for us?" Lisa asked with excitement.

"How wonderful!" Allison said and grinned.

"Now, don't you feel bad for being snappy to me?" Todd asked and winked.

"Buckie, this is so wonderful," Allison said and walked over and kissed Buckie.

"Are we ready to sail?" the boat's captain asked.

"Yes, we're now ready," Buckie said.

"Oh yes! Another exciting Valentine's Day that is full of surprises," Allison said. She and Lisa exchanged a wink and a smile.

Chapter 9

Lisa walked away from Sammie's and Sunshine's table as the server handed the menus to Sammie and Sunshine.

Sunshine studied the cocktail menu. "I'm not sure that I should have any alcohol to drink," Sunshine said. "But these cocktails sound refreshing. So, what does my doctor suggest?"

Sammie smiled and said, "I think that a glass of wine with dinner is okay."

"Perfect. I'll have a glass of red wine," Sunshine replied without hesitation. She looked at Sammie in surprise.

"Isn't that interesting? You know that your preference for wine is red and not white. A start in the right direction," Sammie said and laughed.

Sunshine laughed. "I guess so. I did say red without hesitation."

The Wine Sommelier suggested a perfect red wine to pair with their dinner, and both enjoyed a glass of wine with dinner.

The meal was exquisite. They enjoyed conversations about Sunshine's continued mental health improvement and overall health. Sammie shared more stories of his volunteering at the hospital and his service in the military.

After finishing their dinner, the Pâtissier presented the selection of desserts for the evening. Sammie and Sunshine selected two chocolate desserts.

The hostess walked to the table and asked, "Would you like your desserts served on the balcony? There's a band playing soft music and it's a beautiful night."

"Yes. That would be perfect. Sunshine, do you agree?" Sammie asked.

"Oh yes. That would be lovely," Sunshine replied.

The couple were escorted to a table on the balcony. "Here's a menu of after-dinner drinks and coffees," the hostess said, handing the menu to Sammie.

"Would you like a cup of coffee?" Sammie asked.

"Yes," Sunshine answered.

"Me too," Sammie said.

Sammie ordered the coffee and broke their silence with a question. "Sunshine, when the Travel Director walked over to our table earlier, did she seem familiar to you?"

Sunshine was surprised at the question. "No, not really. But I feel like all faces are familiar. I just can't place them. I saw a woman in the ladies' room earlier, and she sort of looked familiar, but I couldn't place her. She stared at me as if she were surprised to see me. But when I asked if we knew each other, she just rushed out the door. So, I just don't know. I look around here and it all seems familiar, but at the same time, I don't recall how I would have been here."

"I thought the Travel Director ..." Sammie said, removing the card from his shirt pocket. "... Lisa, that was her name ... She said that you looked like someone she knew." He put the card back in his shirt pocket.

"Yes, she did say that," Sunshine said softly.

The conversation was interrupted when the coffees were served. "Desserts are on their way."

They finished desserts, and Sammie requested a taxi be available to take them home. Sammie and Sunshine had a wonderful, relaxing Valentine's Day dinner. They were escorted down to the lobby and were taken to the dock where the water taxi was waiting.

"Thank you," Sammie said to the dock master, and Sammie and Sunshine stepped onto the water taxi.

The ride was only about 20 to 25 minutes, and they soon arrived home. The driver of the water taxi pulled up to the small dock, and Sammie and Sunshine stepped out of the boat onto the dock. Sammie turned and paid the driver. The driver floated the water taxi back from the dock and pulled away.

"Sunshine, you go on inside. I'm going to check and make sure *Happiness* is secured and tied down for the night. I'll see ya inside," Sammie said.

"Okay," Sunshine said and walked inside. She walked to her bedroom and changed into a lightweight sweatshirt and jeans. She removed her turban and was looking in the mirror at the scars on her head when suddenly there was a loud noise. *Were those gunshots?* she thought. She turned and walked out of her bedroom, down the hallway toward the living room, and yelled, "Sammie, what was that?"

When she stepped into the living room, standing in front of her were two masked half-naked men with guns.

She gasped. "What? Who are you?"

"It's not her!" one of the masked men yelled.

"You sure?" the other masked man mumbled.

"Yeah. Sure," he answered.

"No matter. Grab her. We take her," he said in broken English.

Sunshine turned to run when she felt arms wrapping around her waist, and she was grabbed and pulled backward. A handkerchief was forced into her mouth. Her hands were violently pulled behind her back and zip tied. Another handkerchief was tied over her mouth.

Sunshine struggled to get free, but she couldn't. She tried to tell them that she couldn't breathe, but they dragged her out the door and down the steps to their boat. She stumbled as they pushed her into their boat. She saw Rufus lying on the ground. He was shot and appeared dead. She could see Sammie lying face down in his boat. He had been shot. She tried to scream. *They killed him,* she thought. *Dear God, help me!*

The kidnappers forced her to sit down. She shook her head and tried to scream. She could not speak. *I'm going to pass out. I can't…*were her last thoughts, as passed out.

Chapter 10

Sammie slowly opened his eyes. He coughed and groaned as he awoke. He felt excruciating pain through his body, especially his shoulder. *Oh, I hurt,* he thought. *What...who...I...I've been shot.*

Sammie didn't move for a few seconds and listened for sounds of his surroundings. He heard only the splashing of the water against the boat. He tried to get up, but he was too weak. He felt blood trickling over his face. *Where's my phone?* he thought. He couldn't move his left arm. He turned his head and looked across the floor of the boat. He tried to move, but in his fall, his right foot was wedged between the side of the boat and the storage box. His cell phone had fallen out of his pocket and bounced near the boat's starboard floor.

Sammie was able to maneuver his right arm alongside his head. He located his phone lying near his head. He picked up his phone. He raised his head, pushed the button, and said, "Call Corozal Community Hospital."

There was a ringing, and a woman answered the phone. "Corozal Community Hospital. How may I help you?"

"Maria...Maria...This is Dr. Sammie. I've been shot...Send help... On my boat...at home," Sammie said in broken words.

"Dr. Sammie? Is that you? Dr. Sammie?" Maria said in a panic.

"Yes. Hurry. I...I..." Sammie said, and he passed out.

Within an hour, Sammie found himself admitted to the hospital and in a prep room for surgery. Dr. Sanchez was called to come in to perform emergency surgery.

"Sammie, you're going to be okay. The bullet was clean—in and exited. I just need to stitch you up," Dr. Sanchez said slowly as the anesthesiologist administered IV general anesthetic.

Sammie was groggy and groaned.

* * *

The surgery went well, and Sammie was soon admitted and resting in a patient's room for recovery.

The next morning, Sammie was awakened by the nurse entering his room. "Dr. Sammie, how are you feeling this morning?" the nurse asked cheerfully.

"I'm not sure. I feel like I've been shot," Sammie said slowly and drowsily smiled.

The nurse smiled, and asked, "Do you feel like having something to eat? It's almost lunch, but I can fix breakfast for you, or whatever you would like to eat."

"A cup of coffee would be great, and something light, like toast," Sammie replied.

"Coming right up," the nurse said and turned to walk out of the room when Dr. Sanchez walked into the room.

"How's our patient doing?" Dr. Sanchez asked joyfully.

"He's wanting something to eat. So, I think he's doing okay," the nurse replied and exited the room.

"So, as if we don't have enough patients, you become one," Dr. Sanchez said and winked.

"Looks that way," Sammie said.

"Who used you as target practice?" Dr. Sanchez asked.

"Not sure," Sammie said. "Where's Sunshine? Have you heard from her?"

"No. Why?" Dr. Sanchez asked.

"I think she's been kidnapped," Sammie said seriously. "I was checking out my boat, and these two masked men showed up with guns, and without warning, they started shooting."

Sammie hesitated in thought.

"What else do you remember?" Dr. Sanchez asked.

"Well, they said nothing...They just shot me, and seems like I remember hearing Rufus whine, and the next thing I remember is hearing a loud boat motor," Sammie said.

"Dr. Sammie..." Dr. Sanchez hesitated. "Sunshine was not there when medics picked you up. The dog had been shot. After the medics brought you here, they went back and got the dog. They took your dog to the veterinarian for cremation. I'm sorry, but Sunshine was not there."

Sammie stared at Dr. Sanchez. "I don't understand. Who would want to kidnap her? And why?" Sammie asked.

"Dr. Sammie, what if she was the woman...the ex-girlfriend of the cartel? You know, the one that was reported to be missing. What if...?" Dr. Sanchez suggested.

Sammie interrupted Dr. Sanchez, "I don't believe that. She is such a classy and sophisticated, educated lady. Besides, I know she's not."

"How do you know that?" Dr. Sanchez asked.

"I just know," Sammie replied.

"We have to report to the authorities about you being shot. They'll be here this afternoon to question you. You know that we didn't follow protocol on Sunshine's admittance, much less her release, and to tell them that she has been kidnapped...Well, it could look bad on all of us," Dr. Sanchez said.

Sammie didn't answer.

"Here's your cup of coffee, and buttered toast, avocado. This is a good breakfast for you," the nurse said, rolling the food tray cart to his bedside.

"Thank you," Sammie said.

The nurse walked out of the room and Sammie asked Dr. Sanchez, "When can I go home, doc?"

Dr. Sanchez smiled and said, "You're going to have soreness, and I think it's best you stay here until tomorrow."

"How about we compromise? You can take me home at the end of your shift today," Sammie said.

"I'm on all day, so I guess that'll be okay. I'll drive you home this evening," Dr. Sanchez said, walking out of the room. "But remember what I told you about the authorities."

* * *

Sammie was asleep when a nurse walked into his room and gently said, "Dr. Sammie. Wake up. There is someone here to see you."

Sammie stirred and looked up to see two police officers standing in the room.

"Are you awake, Dr. Sammie?" the nurse asked.

Sammie groaned and sat up in bed, and said, "Yes. Thank you."

The nurse walked out of the room.

"We're sorry to disturb you, but we're following up on a report that you suffered a gunshot wound," one of the police officers said. "I'm Officer Mendez, and this is Officer Vega. We have some questions for you."

"Sure," Sammie said.

"Do you know who it was that shot you?" Officer Mendez asked bluntly.

"No," Sammie answered. "There were two masked men with guns. They showed up on a boat."

"Do you know why they would want to harm you?" Officer Vega asked.

"No. And I didn't know them. I had just gotten home from having dinner at the resort and was tending to my boat, and they came out of nowhere and started shooting," Sammie recapped.

"Resort? Beautiful Lady Resort?" Officer Mendez asked.

"Yes," Sammie said."

"Were you dining by yourself?" Officer Vega asked.

"No, I had a lady friend with me," Sammie said.

"Where is she? What happened to her?" Officer Vega asked.

Sammie hesitated, "I don't know. I think the gunman took her. You see…my lady friend has amnesia. And I found her a couple of months ago floating in the water. I brought her here, to the hospital, for treatment, and within a few weeks she was ready to be released, but she still couldn't remember anything before being in the water. So, I suggested that she stay with me until…well…until her memory came back."

"You found her floating in the water? When was this?" Officer Mendez asked and looked over to Officer Vega.

"It was about six or eight weeks ago," Sammie said with no emotion.

"You did not know this woman?" Officer Vega asked.

"No…I had never seen her before," Sammie answered cautiously.

"But you took her to your home when she was released from the hospital?" Office Mendez asked.

"Yes," Sammie replied.

"Why?" Office Vega asked.

"Simply because I found her and knew her treatment in a mental ward wouldn't help her. She has been recuperating at my home, and I see that she goes to all her medical appointments," Sammie explained.

"But you did not know her prior to pulling her from the water?" Office Vega asked.

"No," Sammie said.

"Do you think that was the missing woman?" Officer Vega asked Office Mendez. "You know…the cartel boss's girlfriend?"

Officer Mendez ignored Officer Vega's question.

"I am confused, Mr. Drillenger. That's not protocol. The patient was never reported to authorities. Why was she never reported?" Office Mendez asked.

"It's my fault, and I take full responsibility. I found her, so I felt that I could take care of her. I felt that she shouldn't be in a psych ward. It seemed to be in her best interest," Sammie explained.

"Are you sure you did not know her before finding her in the water?" Officer Vega asked.

"No. I do not know who she is," Sammie said. "I had never seen her before in my life."

"Well ... I suspect that she is the missing girlfriend, and her cartel boyfriend just found her. You were in the crossfire. Is there anything else you remember?" Office Vega said.

"I do remember the boat's name. It was *Black Sword* ... That was the name on the side of the boat," Sammie said.

"That explains it. They're part of the cartel. I guess this case is closed. The girlfriend has been found, and they won't be back. They got what they wanted. And no one was killed, so we're finished here," Officer Mendez said.

"You aren't going to go look for her?" Sammie asked, surprised. "And they did kill my dog."

"I'm sorry about your dog, but there's nothing we can do. She's been taken to Mexico. Her boyfriend is Carlos González at the Hacienda El Rancho. That is out of our jurisdiction. We'll file the report, but ... there's nothing that we can do," Officer Mendez said. "And I suggest you use better judgment next time you recover a floating person in the water with amnesia. The next time, you notify authorities. Do you understand?"

"Yes," Sammie said.

"We hope for your speedy recovery," Officer Vega said, and the officers turned and walked out of the room.

This cannot be happening, Sammie thought. *I have to come up with a plan. Sunshine is in harm's way.*

The nurse walked into Sammie's room and asked, "Are you okay? You look a little flushed."

"Where are my clothes?" Sammie asked, ignoring her question.

"Your clothes are in the closet there, but your shirt was tossed away. Your things were placed in the drawer there," the nurse answered.

"I have an extra shirt in the lounge. Can you get it for me?" Sammie asked.

"Sure," the nurse said, walking out of the room.

Sammie got dressed and opened the drawer, finding his wallet, phone, and Lisa's business card.

Sammie stared at the business card. *Great*, he thought. *I'm going to start with her. I'll call her tomorrow.*

Dr. Sanchez walked into Sammie's room and asked. "All dressed and ready to go?"

"Yes," Sammie answered. "Waiting on my shirt."

"How did the interview go with the authorities?" Dr. Sanchez asked.

"I'll tell you all about it on my way home," Sammie said, smiled, and winked.

Chapter 11

The sun's rays of warmth streamed through a high window onto Sunshine's face. She slowly opened her eyes. *Where am I?* she thought. She remained still and didn't move. Reality hit her. *I've been kidnapped,* she thought. She was surprised to find her hands were no longer zip-tied together and she no longer struggled to breathe.

"You awake now," an attractive young Mexican woman said in broken English. "¿hablas español?"

Sunshine raised and sat on the side of the bed. "No," she answered.

"You do what I tell you," the woman directed. "My name is Carlota, and you do as I say."

"Where am I?" Sunshine asked.

Carlota ignored Sunshine's question. "You take bath. Now," Carlota said and pointed to the bathroom.

"Why?" Sunshine asked.

"Is there a problem, Carlota?" a gruff voice echoed behind the door. The door burst open, and a thug was standing there with a gun.

"No...no, you go away," Carlota said and closed the door.

"You must do as I say. If not, he shoot you," Carlota warned.

Sunshine stood up and walked into the bathroom. The bathroom was exquisite in design and accessories. Carlota tried to assist Sunshine in removing her sweatshirt, and Sunshine pulled away. "I can do it. Are you going to stand there and watch me?" Sunshine asked with irritation.

"Si," Carlota answered coldly.

"I need to pee," Sunshine said defensively.

"You go. I get shower on," Carlota said.

Sunshine heard the water from the shower splashing on the walls and floor. Sunshine moved from the toilet and stepped into the shower.

There were perfume soaps, and the shower was large enough for two people with a unique, stunning animal tile design. She quickly showered and stepped out of the shower. Carlota handed a large fluffy towel to her. Sunshine wrapped herself in the towel.

"Here. Put on," Carlota said. She handed over the clothes that Sunshine had worn the night before to dinner.

"How did you get these?" Sunshine asked, puzzled.

"Yours," Carlota said and smiled. "You put on. I wash others for you."

Sunshine slipped on her top and pants. *Did they go back and get my clothes and help Sammie?* she thought.

"Is my friend here?" Sunshine asked.

Carlota ignored her question.

There was a loud knock on the door and a gruff voice asked, "She dressed?"

"Si. Follow me. Do not run. He shoot you. He kill you. You understand?" Carlota said in a low voice.

The door opened and the thug motioned for them to follow him. He walked in front of Sunshine, and Carlota followed behind Sunshine.

Sunshine could not help but notice as they walked down the long hallway how it was decorated with expensive art pieces and paintings. As they neared the end of the hallway, the thug stepped to the left, which led to an outdoor covered balcony, facing the ocean. There was a long table with flower arrangements placed on the table. A very neatly dressed Mexican man in his early fifties was sitting at the head of the dinner table, and there was a place setting at the other end.

"You sit," Carlota said and pointed to the chair. The thug motioned with the gun for her to sit.

"Carlota, bring our guest water, coffee, juice, and toast. Would you like anything else?" the Mexican man asked kindly.

Sunshine shook her head "no" and sat down.

"I am thirsty," Sunshine said calmly.

"Perfect," he said. "At once, Carlota, and I will have another cup of coffee."

"Si. Right away," Carlota said.

"My name is Carlos González," he said to Sunshine. "You are my guest."

"Where am I?" Sunshine asked slowly.

"You are here at my Hacienda El Rancho," Carlos answered.

"In Mexico?" Sunshine asked. "Why am I here?"

"Oh, here is your food," Carlos said.

Carlota set down a cup of coffee in front of Carlos and then served the food and drinks to Sunshine. The thug stood behind Sunshine's chair and watched.

Sunshine was so thirsty that she drank all of the water in the glass. "May I have another?" she asked.

Carlota looked to Carlos. He nodded yes.

"Why am I here?" Sunshine asked again.

"You are my guest," Carlos said. "And I don't want to hurt you. I don't want you to feel afraid."

"Your thugs killed my friend," said Sunshine harshly.

"Yes...an unfortunate mistake. But we do not know that he is dead. My associates went back for your clothes, and he was not there. So, you see, we do not know if he is alive or dead. We'll think that he is alive," Carlos said condescendingly.

Sunshine stared at Carlos and took a small bite of the toast.

"Why am I here?" Sunshine asked again.

Carlos didn't answer her question, but asked her, "What is your name?"

Sunshine panicked. *Oh no, he's not going to believe me when I tell him that I don't know my name,* she thought.

"You hesitate," Carlos said. "Tell me your name."

"My name is ... Sunshine," she said.

The thug snickered. Carlos glanced a harsh look at the thug and the thug quickly stopped snickering.

"Sunshine is not a name. It is ... a ... how you say? Nickname," Carlos said. "So, I ask you again, what is your name? I know it isn't Christina. You see, my associates heard that my ... well ... my girlfriend, who somehow disappeared, was spotted nearby. So, I, of course, wanted to see her. And I sent them to find her. They came back with you. And, I will admit, at first, I was very disappointed. However, you looked familiar. And I couldn't help but think that we had met before. I just needed to think about it to be able to recall."

"I don't know you," Sunshine said confidently.

"Oh, but I do know you," Carlos said firmly. He looked at the thug and said, "Bring me the folder."

The thug stepped out of sight and quickly returned with a manila folder and placed it on the table in front of Carlos. Carlos placed his hand on the folder.

Carlos looked back toward Sunshine and said, "Now ... once more ... what is your name?"

Sunshine swallowed hard and tears filled her eyes, her hands began to tremble, and she spoke slowly. "I do not know my name. I was in a boating accident several weeks ago ... and I haven't been able to recall anything before the accident. I don't know my name or ..." Sunshine couldn't finish her sentence. She choked on her tears.

Carlos sat and watched her, showing no emotion.

Sunshine took a sip of water and looked at Carlos. "You don't have to believe me, but I have no reason to lie. I do not know you and I don't understand what's going on here," she said in a panic-stricken tone.

Carlos studied Sunshine closely and said, "I think I believe you. But I do know your name. I know who you are."

Sunshine gasped and asked, "How do you know me?"

Carlos removed a photo from the folder and motioned to the thug to take it to Sunshine. The thug quickly placed the photo on the table in front of her.

"Who do you see in the picture?" Carlos asked.

Sunshine looked closely at the photo. It was a black-and-white photo of a woman. She was shocked when she saw it. She recognized herself in the picture.

"Do you recognize that person?" Carlos asked.

Sunshine looked at the photo and back at Carlos. "That is me. Why do you have a picture of me?"

"So, what is your name?" Carlos asked.

Sunshine looked at the picture and concentrated. She shook her head and said in disbelief, "I can't recall my name."

"Your name is Jan," Carlos said.

Sunshine looked at Carlos and asked, "My name is Jan?"

"Yes. Jan Foster," Carlos said.

Sunshine looked at the picture and felt confused. She looked back at Carlos and said, "I don't know you, and why should I believe you? How do you have a picture of me? And how do you know my name?"

Carlos took out another photo from the folder and motioned for the thug to hand it to Sunshine.

The thug took that photo and placed it next photo to the first photo. The second photo was a picture of four adults. There were two men and two women. Sunshine recognized herself, and the other woman looked familiar.

"Do you recognize anyone in the photo?" Carlos asked seriously.

"That's me with three other people," Sunshine said slowly.

"Do you recognize anyone else in the photo?" Carlos asked.

"No," she answered and continued to study the photo. "I think that I saw that woman at the resort. My friend…the one your thugs killed… He and I had a Valentine's Day dinner there, and I think that I saw her there," Sunshine finished with uncertainty. "But I'm not sure."

"Really?" Carlos asked and was surprised. "Interesting. Is that the only one you recognize?"

"Yes," Sunshine answered. "I…I don't know. I can't remember. Why do you have these pictures?"

"Look closely. You do not know the men in the photo?" Carlos asked.

Sunshine studied the photos carefully. She touched them and ran her fingers over the photos. "No," Sunshine said.

"You should. The two men are brothers. The man next to you there is your boyfriend. And the other man is his brother. He is with his girl-friend," Carlos explained. "Now, when was the last time you saw your boyfriend?"

Sunshine swallowed hard. She felt faint. Her thoughts were spin-ning. *Is that the woman I saw in the ladies' room? Is that man my boyfriend? Where is he now? Is this gangster telling me the truth?*

"I don't feel well," Sunshine said softly. "I think that I'm going to pass out."

Without warning, Sunshine passed out, slumping in her chair and leaning toward the floor. Carlota was standing beside her chair and grabbed Sunshine before she hit the floor.

"She out," Carlota said in broken English, holding Sunshine in her arms.

"Take her to her room. We will let our guest rest," Carlos instructed the thug. "And you return to me for instructions."

The thug carried Sunshine to the bedroom and walked out of the room as Carlota removed Sunshine's clothing and slipped a soft cotton nightgown on her limp body.

"You have instructions for me?" the thug, Raff, said. He walked towards Carlos and his comrade, Emilo, who was standing in the room.

"Yes. You and your comrade here brought me a diamond in the rough. However, you have made a grave mistake in shooting her friend. I need to know if he is alive or dead. And if he's alive, bring him to me. Do you understand? Do not kill him," Carlos demanded.

"What if he is dead?" Emilo asked.

"The two of you should not return," Carlos said coldly.

Raff and Emilo glanced at each other and nodded and walked out of the room.

Chapter 12

On the way home from the hospital, Dr. Sanchez stopped by the veterinarian's office so that Sammie could pick up the tiny urn of Rufus's remains.

"Thanks," Sammie said as he opened the car door and sat down. "This dog meant the world to me. He didn't deserve this."

"No, and you didn't either," Dr. Sanchez said.

"What do you think they'll do to Sunshine?" Sammie asked with concern.

"I don't know. When he realizes that she's not the girlfriend…who knows…they may just bring her back," Dr. Sanchez said.

"Not without a ransom," Sammie said. "So, you don't think she's the girlfriend either, do you?"

"You've convinced me. But you didn't convince the authorities," Dr. Sanchez said. "They believe that the woman kidnapped is the girlfriend. So, what are you going to do?"

"According to the authorities, the woman was taken to Carlos González, in Mexico, so that's the starting point," Sammie said.

"On your own?" Dr. Sanchez asked.

"Not sure," Sammie said. "But I am going to find her."

"Here we are," Dr. Sanchez said as he drove into Sammie's driveway.

"Thank you," Sammie said, stepping out of the car. "It's good to be home."

"Dr. Sammie, I hope you understand what I'm about to say," Dr. Sanchez said seriously. "I cannot help you go after Sunshine. With my family, I cannot take the risk. I hope you understand."

"Of course, I do. Just be available when I need a good doctor," Sammie said with a tone of humor.

"That I can do," Dr. Sanchez said and drove away.

Sammie walked inside. He was surprised to find his home ransacked. The gun that was inside near the front door was gone. Clothes were scattered all over the floor. It looked like most of Sunshine's clothes were missing.

Sammie rushed to his closet, pushed back his clothes, and opened the hidden door. He was relieved to see that his safe was still locked and had not been located. He opened it and took out a pistol, ammunition, and an SR-16 rifle. He locked the safe, closed the door, and pushed clothes against it.

He walked to his bedroom, and from his desk took out the newspaper clipping with Sunshine's picture. He walked to the kitchen and reached for Lisa's business card in his wallet. He placed it on the counter next to the newspaper clipping. *She knows something*, he thought.

He picked up his cell phone and dialed Lisa's phone number. To his surprise, Lisa answered the phone, "Lisa speaking."

"Hi, Lisa. This is Dr. Sammie Drillenger. We met on Valentine's Day…My friend, Sunshine, and I were having dinner there and you…" Sammie was interrupted by Lisa.

"Oh yes. I remember. I hope you had an enjoyable time. How can I help you?" Lisa said.

"I wanted to see if it's possible to set a time to meet with you and discuss plans for a family reunion and how we can make arrangements. Would you have time tomorrow to meet?" Sammie asked.

"Tomorrow? Let me check my schedule here," Lisa said. "In the morning, would 11:00 a.m. be a good time for you?"

"Perfect. I'll see you then," Sammie said.

"Great. I'll meet you on the main dock at 11:00 a.m.," Lisa confirmed.

"Thank you," Sammie said. "See you tomorrow." Sammie ended the phone conversation.

Lisa hung up the phone and thought, *Wonder if Sunshine will be joining him.*

Sammie grabbed a bucket, filled it with soapy water, and walked out to his boat. He washed away the blood stains the best he could with one arm. As he cleaned, he relived the evening he was shot and tried to recall every detail. It was just a blur.

It was getting late, so he decided to go to bed to get rest. He was hopeful that the meeting with Lisa would provide answers.

It was almost 3:00 a.m. when Sammie was awakened by what he thought was a boat motor shutting off. He grabbed the pistol under his pillow, leaving the rifle in bed, and eased out of his bed, out of the bedroom, and out the backdoor leading to the patio. He tiptoed around the corner of the house and peeked around the corner. He saw the boat. By the moonlight, he saw the name on the boat, *Black Sword.*

Sammie dropped to the ground and crawled to the edge of the front porch. He watched the two thugs ease out of their boat. They slipped quietly up the steps and jiggled the doorknob. The door opened. They slowly stepped inside. Without warning, Sammie jumped upon the porch and stormed through the doorway. "Drop 'em. Drop 'em or die where you stand!" Sammie yelled.

One of the thugs pointed his gun at Sammie. "I kill you," he said.

"No, he need to be alive!" the other thug yelled in broken English.

"Drop 'em! Now! Slowly!" Sammie yelled.

The thugs, Raff and Emilo, laid their guns down on the floor. "And the guns in your belts," Sammie instructed. Sammie motioned to them with his gun. "You understand me. All guns on the floor."

Reluctantly, they put the other guns on the floor.

"Hands in the air! Keep 'em high! Now…where is the woman you kidnapped? The one you forced to go with you," Sammie asked.

Raff and Emilo glanced at each other, but neither answered.

"Die here and now, or tell me where the woman is," Sammie yelled.

"She at Hacienda El Rancho," Raff answered slowly in poor English.

"Why?" Sammie asked.

Neither answered.

"I'm not going to ask again," Sammie said sharply. "Tell me."

They looked at each other and nodded. "Us thought she Mendez girlfriend ... alive ... suppose dead ... but alive. But it not her," Emilo said in broken English. "He want you now."

"I see. Okay. Out the door. March ... now. Move!" Sammie firmly instructed. "Time for a boat ride."

Both Raff and Emilo walked out the door and down the steps to their boat. "Get in the boat. One at a time. Hands in the air!" Sammie said. "Slowly!"

Raff stepped into the boat first and Emilo followed him. "Keep those hands high in the air!" Sammie said. "Now, turn around."

Each one turned around slowly, facing Sammie.

"Which one of you shot my dog?" Sammie asked coldly.

Neither one answered. "I asked, which one of you killed my dog?" Sammie asked slowly.

Raff laughed and said proudly, "I did."

Sammie quickly pointed his pistol at Raff's head and pulled the trigger. Raff collapsed. Emilo lunged to the edge of the boat to jump in the water, but Sammie pulled the trigger without hesitation and shot Emilo in the back of the head. He fell backward inside the boat. "Guess you were the one who shot me," Sammie said out loud.

Sammie walked over to the edge of the boat. He stared at Raff and Emilo. He raised his gun and shot each one of them again as they lay motionless.

Sammie rushed inside, got dressed, and retrieved the rifle from his bed, and retrieved a grenade from his safe. He picked up the guns off the floor and hurried back to their boat. He threw the thugs' guns into their boat, landing on their dead bodies.

Sammie used a pull line and hooked their boat to his boat. He slowly moved his boat out into the water, pulling the boat, *Black Sword*, behind his. He slowly and meticulously maneuvered both boats into the ocean water. In complete darkness, Sammie released his boat and drifted away from *Black Sword*. He was several yards away and took out the grenade and threw it onto the boat. He quickly sped away, and within seconds, *Black Sword* exploded, sending debris and haze in the air and everywhere. Large waves tossed Sammie's boat violently, but Sammie was able to control the boat as he sped away in the darkness. Sammie was coasting his boat into the cove to his dock when, at a distance, he heard sirens from the Coast Guard rushing to the explosion.

Sammie finally arrived home, docked his boat, walked inside, and put away his gun. He showered and went to bed to rest for a few hours before he met with Lisa. He was sure he had done the right thing. He would kill anyone who got in his way of rescuing Sunshine, and now, he knew for sure who had kidnapped her.

Chapter 13

Lisa was excited about meeting Sammie. She was waiting on the dock when Sammie pulled his small boat up to the dock.

"Welcome," the dock master said. "Will you be visiting for a few days?"

"I have an appointment with Lisa . . ." Sammie said when he was interrupted.

"Hi, Sammie, welcome," Lisa said and extended her hand.

"Yes, I'm happy that you could meet with me," Sammie said and shook her hand.

"We'll ride up to the hotel and talk in the restaurant," Lisa said.

"Perfect," Sammie said, and both sat on the cart.

"Sammie, looks like you had an accident," Lisa said, observing his arm in a sling and making small talk as they were escorted to the hotel.

"Yes, but healing quickly," Sammie said.

"Did you and your lady companion enjoy your dinner?" Lisa asked.

"Oh yes, it was exquisite and wonderful," Sammie replied.

"I was hoping that she would be joining us today," Lisa said, fishing for information.

"Maybe another time," Sammie said and smiled.

"Here we are. Just follow me, and we'll sit in the restaurant. Would you like something to eat? Breakfast or lunch, light bite?" Lisa said as they walked into the restaurant.

"Unsweet tea would be perfect," Sammie replied.

Lisa motioned to the hostess as she and Sammie sat down at a table located at the far end of the restaurant.

"Two unsweet teas and chocolate chip cookies please," Lisa ordered.

"Got it," the hostess said.

"Now, tell me Sammie, what do you have in mind for this family reunion? What's the time frame?" Lisa asked earnestly.

Sammie hesitated. "I do want to …"

Sammie was interrupted by the hostess. "Here are your teas. I hope that you like spice cinnamon-flavored tea with homemade chocolate chip cookies."

"Yes. Thank you," Sammie said.

Lisa nodded.

Sammie took a sip of his tea. "Very good," he said.

"Glad you like it," Lisa said. "Now, about your family reunion."

Sammie lowered his head and removed the newspaper clipping from his pocket. He looked up to Lisa and said, "I got this meeting under false pretense."

Lisa did not respond. She watched Sammie as he unfolded the newspaper clipping. He placed it open on the table. Lisa looked down at the clipping.

"You are in this picture with Sunshine. I need to know about her. What is her name? Where is she from? Tell me," Sammie methodically instructed.

Lisa picked up the newspaper clipping but never answered.

"What's her name? Can you tell me?" Sammie asked.

Lisa paused and laid the newspaper back on the table.

Lisa took a deep breath. "Her name is Jan Foster," Lisa said slowly. "Why don't you know her name?"

"She was in a boating accident, and I rescued her. She has amnesia and doesn't recall anything beyond me pulling her onto my boat."

Lisa stayed silent.

"It is obvious that she was here. Was she a guest here?" Sammie asked.

Lisa looked at the newspaper clipping again and looked back at Sammie.

"You found her floating in the water?" Lisa asked.

"Yes. Now, what is it that you are not telling me?" Sammie asked sternly.

There was an awkward silence.

Lisa broke the silence and said slowly, "Her name is Jan Foster."

"And where is she from? Obviously, she was a guest here. Is the other woman her sister? Is she married? I have so many questions," Sammie asked.

"I can't tell you much more without knowing more about you," Lisa said firmly. "How do you know her?"

Sammie smiled. "I told you. On the day after Christmas, that night around midnight, I found her floating in the water, barely alive. She was near death. She had lost a lot of blood. I took her to the hospital for care. She improved except for her memory. She doesn't recall anything before being pulled out of the water. Now...you tell me what you know," Sammie said.

Lisa studied Sammie's face and didn't say anything.

"Lisa, Sunshine—Jan, as you called her—is in danger. I need help. She's been kidnapped," Sammie said calmly.

Lisa gasped. "Kidnapped? What do you mean?"

"A Mexican cartel's girlfriend went missing, and somehow it was thought that Sunshine was the missing woman, and these two thugs showed up at my home...shot me...and kidnapped her. That's how I ended up with my arm in a sling. I was shot. Now, you have to help me. I need to know as much you can tell me so I can get her out of danger," Sammie shared.

"I need you to wait here. Wait here. I'm going to have you meet someone who can help you," Lisa instructed. "Don't leave. It may take me a few minutes, okay?"

"Okay. Who am I meeting?" Sammie asked.

"Just wait here," Lisa repeated.

Lisa walked to the hallway and texted Winston, Buckie, and Allison.

Lisa: 911 meeting now

Allison: Where?

Lisa: Meet in office

Allison: On way

Winston: Now?

Lisa: Yes on way

Buckie: In office now

Lisa walked back to the table where Sammie was sitting. "Let's go," Lisa said.

"Where are we going?" Sammie asked as he stood.

"I want you to meet the owners of this resort. They can provide details. Follow me," Lisa said coldly.

Lisa and Sammie rode the elevator to the top floor. The receptionist greeted Lisa. "They're expecting us," Lisa said.

Two double doors opened, and they were in the large greeting room of Winston's residence. Allison was sitting on the sofa and was having a drink. Henry stood behind the bar and Buckie was sitting at the end of the long bar. Winston rounded the corner into the greeting room.

"Sammie, have a seat please," Lisa instructed, motioning for him to sit on the sofa.

Sammie walked over and sat down. He was amazed at the views and the entire room. It had a full bar, a large meeting table, and a long sofa. It was a living room that served as a full-size office. The windows were open to a large balcony that blended into the endless ocean views.

"Hi, everyone," Lisa said. "This Sammie."

Sammie interjected, "Samuel Drillenger, retired M.D., and yes, please call me Sammie."

Lisa continued, "This is Winston, and this is Buckie. They are the resort owners. This is Henry, our in-house bartender, and this is Buckie's fiancée, Allison."

Everyone exchanges handshakes.

"So, what's the emergency here?" Winston asked seriously.

Lisa had her phone in her hand and scrolled through until she located the photo she had taken of Sammie and Sunshine having dinner. She handed the phone to Winston.

"Do you recognize the woman?" Lisa asked smugly.

Winston stared at the photo. He gasped and collapsed onto a bar stool. He went pale. He was motionless. He threw the phone to Lisa.

"What a sick joke," Winston said harshly.

"Winston!" Lisa snapped and caught her phone in mid-air. "It is no joke!"

"What's going on?" Buckie asked.

Lisa scrolled back through, located the photo, and handed the phone to Buckie. "Don't throw my phone to me like Winston," Lisa instructed.

"Henry, fix me a double on the rocks," Winston said. "That's not her."

"I know it's her," Allison interjected. "I saw her in the bathroom. I recognized her but she didn't recognize me."

"What do you mean, you saw her in the bathroom?" Winston asked. "When? How?"

"The evening that the photo was taken, she was coming into the ladies' room when I was leaving. She acted like she should know me, but she didn't recognize me," Allison explained.

"It's not her," Winston said in denial.

"Yup, it's her. So, I want to know ... Whose body did you identify as being Jan?" Buckie asked, staring at the photo.

"Yes. That's what I would like to know," Allison said abruptly. "Who did I take back to Virginia and have a service for?"

"I probably can help you with that," Sammie interjected after being very quiet and listening to the conversation.

"Really?" Allison asked sarcastically.

"That was the same night the girlfriend of a Mexican cartel boss in Mexico disappeared. So, maybe you identified the wrong woman," Sammie suggested.

"How could that happen?" Buckie asked. "Winston identified the body...You did identify the body, didn't you?"

Winston sat with a blank stare.

"Winston, tell me. Did you look at the body?" Buckie demanded to know.

"Obviously not," Lisa snapped.

Winston hesitated and slowly answered, "I was so upset. The love of my life was dead. And it was my fault. She fell overboard and I couldn't grab her. I didn't want to believe that after all this time...We were so close to getting back together...I believed that she would accept every-thing. I was so upset—"

Buckie interrupted Winston, "So, you didn't actually look at the body, did you?"

"No," Winston replied. "I saw a woman's arm hanging off the table and the body was covered with a sheet. I just assumed it was her. The Coast Guard indicated that it must be her. So, I assumed it was her."

"Well, the story's going to get better," Lisa said sarcastically. "Jan has been kidnapped...by the cartel."

"The Mexican cartel?" Buckie yelled. "What do you mean?"

Winston became excited and interrupted, "Kidnapped! By the Mexican cartel? Do you mean Carlos González?"

"We're dead," Buckie whispered under his breath. "Henry, fix me a double."

Surprised, Sammie said, "I'm confused here. You two know Carlos González? You're familiar with the cartel. You two are drug dealers?"

"No," Winston said.

Sammie interrupted Winston, "Sunshine is kidnapped because of the two of you?"

"No. It's nothing like that," Winston replied. "It's...it's..."

"Don't tell him anything, "Buckie warned rudely. "We don't know who this joker is. For all we know, he's part of the cartel."

Sammie stood, walked over to Buckie, and started a face-to-face argument. "Me? I'm not part of the problem here. You are. How dare you accuse me of doing what you and your brother have obviously been doing. It's because of the two of you that Sunshine is in danger!"

Sammie raised his fist when Lisa grabbed and pulled strongly on his arm. "Sammie, sit down! Calm down!"

Winston rushed over and took ahold of Sammie's arm and calmly said, "Man, just calm down. I'll explain. Just calm down. And her name is Jan."

Sammie took a step back. He took a deep breath. He looked at Winston and demanded, "Explain now. Her name is Sunshine. You start explaining ...now!"

"He can't know," Buckie insisted. "It'll complicate things. I'm telling you."

Winston ignored Buckie and said, "Several years ago, we helped launder money for him. Carlos. And we lost touch with him when we quit."

"How did you just walk away? I hear that it doesn't work that way. And you lived to tell about it?" Sammie snapped.

"Sit down," Winston said. "We only walked away because we had plastic surgery to change our appearance. Therefore, I don't think Carlos González could link Jan to us."

"But you don't know that, do you?" Sammie asked directly as he sat down.

There was silence. Winston never answered the question.

Allison broke the silence. "What are we going to do?"

Winston hesitated and replied, "I think you, Buckie and Lisa, should return to the States. Buckie, you start closing our bank accounts and transferring funds to our Swiss accounts. And Sammie...you and I are going to go rescue Jan."

Sammie slowly stood, turned, and walked toward the door. He looked back to Winston and said, "No. You and I are not going to rescue Jan. You're part of the problem here...you and your brother. I'm going alone."

As he walked out the door, Lisa yelled, "No, wait!"

"Let him go," Winston said sadly. "He's in love with her, too."

Chapter 14

Back at the Hacienda

"Carlota, when is your brother to arrive?" Carlos asked. "And I want my usual breakfast served on the balcony this morning. And check on our guest."

"Half-brother, and soon," Carlota replied.

"Boat or car?" Carlos asked.

"Car," Carlota yelled as she walked to Sunshine's room.

Carlota unlocked the door to the Sunshine's room and peeked through the opened door. Sunshine appeared to be asleep. Carlota slowly closed the door and locked it. She walked downstairs to the kitchen, prepared the light brunch for Carlos, and picked up the newspaper that had been placed on the kitchen table.

Carlos was patiently sitting at the end of the long table on the balcony. Carlota carried the food upstairs and placed his food on the table and poured his coffee. Carlos handed her a piece of fruit to eat. She took the fruit and chewed it and swallowed it, then smiled.

Carlos nodded. Carlota placed the newspaper on the table in front of Carlos.

"How's our guest doing?" Carlos asked, opening the pages of the newspaper.

"Sleeping," Carlota answered.

"When the doctor arrives …" Carlos was interrupted by a call that came across his walkie-talkie.

"Sir, Dr. Sanchez is here. He claims you called him."

"Yes. Escort him to the front door," Carlos ordered.

"Carlota, greet our doctor. Bring him to me," Carlos instructed.

Carlota rushed downstairs to the front door and greeted Dr. Sanchez at the front entrance with two bodyguards watching his every move.

Carlota greeted Dr. Sanchez. "Thank you for coming," she said and hugged him.

"Did I really have a choice?" Dr. Sanchez whispered in her ear.

Carlota looked at Dr. Sanchez, smiled, and shook her head no. "Carlos would like for you to join him on the balcony."

"Perfect," Dr. Sanchez said, following Carlota up the stairs from the foyer and down the hallway to the opened doors, leading to the balcony.

Carlos stood and greeted Dr. Sanchez with a handshake and hug.

"So good to see you," Carlos said.

"Thank you," Dr. Sanchez said coldly.

"I have a guest who needs your attention. A woman. She claims she has amnesia," Carlos explained.

Dr. Sanchez tried not to look surprised. He knew it was Sunshine. "Why do you think that she is not telling you the truth?" Dr. Sanchez asked professionally.

"I showed her this picture," Carlos said, pointing to the picture lying on the table. "She recognized herself, but she claimed did not recall her name. And she claimed she didn't recognize anyone else in the photo."

Dr. Sanchez picked up the picture and looked at it closely. He recognized Allison but didn't acknowledge it. He placed the photo on the table and asked, "But she did recognize herself?"

"Yes," Carlos replied.

"I'll see what I can do," Dr. Sanchez said. "But I am not skilled in this type of medical situation. You do know that?"

"I know. But you're family," Carlos said and grinned.

Dr. Sanchez snickered and said, "Not exactly, and you and I do travel in different circles."

There was silence.

"Where is your…guest and my patient?" Dr. Sanchez asked, breaking the awkward silence.

"Carlota, show Dr. Sanchez to our guest," Carlos said and smiled.

Carlota motioned for Dr. Sanchez to follow her. Dr. Sanchez nodded and did so. They walked down the hallway to Sunshine's room.

Carlota opened the door and whispered, "I believe she's ill. I believe she has no memory."

Dr. Sanchez smiled and walked into the room. "Sunshine," Dr. Sanchez said softly. "Wake up."

Sunshine slowly awoke and looked around the room. She was surprised when she saw Dr. Sanchez standing near her bed.

"Dr. Sanchez? Is that you? What are you doing here?" Sunshine asked.

"It's okay," Dr. Sanchez said. "Carlota, leave me alone with your guest."

"I not sure I can," Carlota said in broken English.

"It's okay. I'll take responsibility," Dr. Sanchez said and assured Carlota. "And she needs food. Go prepare a light meal for her. You can do that, can't you?"

"Yes," Carlota answered and walked out of the room, locking the door behind her. Dr. Sanchez waited until the door clicked.

"Sunshine, I'm here to evaluate your health," Dr. Sanchez said quietly.

"You're a drug dealer?" Sunshine asked with disappointment.

"No. Carlota is my half-sister, and her boss, Carlos, asked that I examine you. He's unsure that you have amnesia," Dr. Sanchez explained. "He's wanting some information from you, so he wanted me to examine you to confirm that you do have amnesia."

"He killed Sammie," Sunshine said with sadness in her voice and tears in her eyes. "Did you know that?"

"No, Sammie isn't dead. He was shot, and Carlos probably thinks that Sammie is dead, but he isn't. Sammie's worried about you, and he's trying to come up with a plan to rescue you," Dr. Sanchez shared. "Sammie is sick with worry over you."

"He's not dead?" Sunshine asked. "Are you sure?"

"He's fine. Now, let's talk about you. Are you okay?" Dr. Sanchez asked.

"I don't understand why I'm here. Carlos showed me a photo and told me that my name is Jan Foster. When I try to think about it, I get dizzy and feel nauseated. What's going on? Why am I here? I'm so scared. I am afraid of Carlos. I think he will kill me if I don't tell him who those people are in the pictures, and I don't know who they are," Sunshine said through tears.

"Stay calm. I have a plan, but you'll have to trust me. Will you trust me?" Dr. Sanchez asked seriously.

Sunshine hesitated. She stared at Dr. Sanchez. "I don't think that I have a choice," she replied. "But how are you going to help me?"

"First, you're going to have to be calm ...no matter what happens," Dr. Sanchez warned. "I'll assure Carlos that you do have amnesia and will suggest to him to have another doctor examine you. Just be patient and remain calm. Can you do that?"

"I'll try," Sunshine answered. "Who is the other doctor?"

"It'll be Sammie," Dr. Sanchez whispered. "But you must..." Dr. Sanchez was interrupted by the clicking of the locked door.

"I brought food and drink," Carlota announced as she placed the food on the table.

"Perfect," Dr. Sanchez said. "And I'm finished here and will talk to Carlos. Eat and rest," he said to Sunshine.

Sunshine gave a weak smile and said, "Okay."

Dr. Sanchez and Carlota exited the room.

"Carlota, are you happy here?" Dr. Sanchez whispered to her as they walked down the hallway.

Carlota stopped, looked at Dr. Sanchez, and answered, "My best friend was his wife. We grew up together. She helped me get this job. I liked working here when she was alive, but not now. Carlos threatens me, and I'm afraid for him. I can't leave. He kill me."

"But if you had a chance to leave, would you?" Dr. Sanchez asked.

"Yes. But where would I go?" Carlota asked.

"Be brave," Dr. Sanchez said, turned, and continued to walk down the hallway to the balcony where Carlos was sitting and reading the newspaper.

"Come in. What is your report on our guest?" Carlos pointedly asked.

"She's telling you the truth. She does have amnesia," Dr. Sanchez said.

"Ah…you have seen my guest before?" Carlos asked.

"Yes. She was brought to the hospital just after the Christmas holiday. She had been pulled from the water. It appeared that she had fallen overboard. She was admitted and released, but her memories have not returned. I am hopeful, because physically she's improving," Dr. Sanchez said. "But for now, she doesn't recall anything beyond being pulled from the water. But there was another doctor who assisted with her wounds and psychological treatment. That is not my training."

"Another doctor?" Carlos asked.

"Yes. If you think it will help, I can arrange for him to examine your guest," Dr. Sanchez volunteered.

"Look at this photo in the paper," Carlos said, pointing at the photo in the newspaper. "The photo shows pieces of a boat, and see there…Right there…See …See the word *sword*…Someone killed my associates."

Dr. Sanchez did not comment as he studied the photo in the newspaper. Carlos placed another photo on top.

"I need to find these two men. She is here with her boyfriend," Carlos said as he looked at the photo. "They stole my money. I want my money."

Dr. Sanchez picked up the photo, looking at it closely, and asked, "When was this photo taken?"

"About seven or eight years ago," Carlos said. "She has changed very little. It is her in this photo. Her name is Jan Foster. She must remember. I have no use for her if she cannot tell me where they are."

Dr. Sanchez understood the underlying message. Carlos would kill her. "She cannot help you for now, but her condition requires care. Let me arrange for the other doctor to examine her. It may prove to be helpful," Dr. Sanchez said calmly and placed the photo on the table.

Carlos padded the photo. He sat quietly for a moment, then said, "Okay. I trust you. I will have Carlota coordinate his visit. You may go now."

"Thank you. I will await to hear from Carlota," Dr. Sanchez replied.

Carlos motioned to Carlota to escort Dr. Sanchez to the door, to leave the property.

Chapter 15

Dr. Sanchez was almost home when he decided to call Dr. Sammie from his cell phone.

"Hi, how are you doing?" Dr. Sammie answered.

"Good. You?" Dr. Sanchez said.

"I had an interesting meeting today, and I want to share it with you. Are you needing help at the hospital? I can run by there," Dr. Sammie said.

"No. I need to come and see you. I have some information about Sunshine. I don't want to discuss it over the phone, so. It's important that I meet with you. I'm on call tonight at the hospital, but I can run by your house and be there in about an hour. Can you do that?" Dr. Sanchez asked.

"Yes. Sunshine…is she okay? You can't talk about it over the phone?" Dr. Sammie asked.

"No. I'll see you in about an hour," Dr. Sanchez said and abruptly ended the call.

* * *

Dr. Sanchez arrived at Dr. Sammie's home in less than an hour. Sammie heard him drive into the driveway and yelled out from the back deck, "Hey, around here."

Dr. Sanchez walked around to the back of house and entered the deck area.

"I hope you're hungry. I got the fish and shrimp grillin', and they're almost ready to eat," Dr. Sammie said proudly. "Do you want a beer?"

"Well, I am hungry…but I guess I better not have a beer. How about iced tea?" Dr. Sanchez said.

Dr. Sammie walked to the kitchen and returned with an iced tea for Dr. Sanchez. Dr. Sammie sipped on a beer.

He handed the iced tea to Dr. Sanchez and asked, "What's this about…Sunshine?"

Dr. Sanchez sat down, and Dr. Sammie tended to the food on the grill.

"I saw her today," Dr. Sanchez said slowly.

Dr. Sammie almost dropped the plate with the grilled fish and shrimp. "You what?" Dr. Sammie asked in shock. "You saw her?"

"Yes. She's okay, but she is being held at Carlos's Hacienda," Dr. Sanchez said cautiously.

Surprised, Dr. Sammie asked, "How do you know this?"

"My half-sister works for Carlos. Carlota became best friends with Carlos's first wife throughout school. Later in life, Carlota went through a nasty divorce and basically ended up homeless. Carlos's wife suggested that Carlota come to work for her as her assistant. Carlos agreed…and Carlota was very happy there until about three years ago, when Carlos's wife died in a helicopter crash. It was a real accident…He had nothing to do with it. The pilot got into bad weather, must have gotten disoriented, and crashed. And, of course, Carlos knows that Carlota's half-brother is a doctor, and if he has a minor situation that he wants checked out and kept off the grid, he calls me," Dr. Sanchez explained.

Dr. Sammie placed the food onto plates set on the table and sat down.

"I thought that you wanted nothing to do with him," Dr. Sammie said bitterly.

"I don't. And I've made it clear that I want no part of his activities. He understands that he and I are on opposite tracks of life. I want nothing to do with his illegal activities or drugs. He has respected that. He rarely calls upon me, but once in a while, he does," Dr. Sanchez said. "He wanted me to come and see who he called 'his guest' for a medical evaluation. He wanted me to confirm that his guest, Sunshine, has amnesia."

"Amnesia? Of course she does! His guest is being held against her will, and you know that," Dr. Sammie said harshly. "She's not a guest. You left her there in harm's way!"

"I know it may look that way, but Dr. Sammie, I could not just walk in and take her out of there. There are bodyguards and guns everywhere. Besides, I don't want my family to be put at risk. Do you understand that?" Dr. Sanchez asked.

"Why didn't you take me with you? You knew that his guest was Sunshine. I could have gotten her out of there," Dr. Sammie said abruptly.

"And how would you have done that? Shoot everyone? You couldn't have gotten her out of there any more than I could have. And, if you had been with me, that would've put us all in a compromising position. Carlos would have killed us all. He is a dangerous man," Dr. Sanchez said sadly.

"But Sunshine is still here. Is she okay? What's he going to do to her? She's in the household with this man that you just said is dangerous," Dr. Sammie said angrily.

"Stay calm. I have a plan, and it does include you. I have a plan for you ... not me ... but you to get her out of there. It will be a big risk," Dr. Sanchez said.

"A plan? How can I trust you? Maybe it's a plan to get Sunshine and me killed!" Dr. Sammie said loudly.

Dr. Sanchez took a bite of food and a sip of his of tea. He remained calm and slowly said, "Would I be here if I didn't care about her ... and you? I don't have to be here. So, yes, trust me. I have a plan."

Dr. Sammie took a sip of his beer, inhaled a deep breath, and said, "Okay. What is it?"

"Sunshine doesn't have her memory, but Carlos has a photo that was taken of her and two men and other woman. He wants to find the men 'cause he claims that they stole money from him. He also said that one of the men in the photo is her boyfriend …" Dr. Sanchez was interrupted by Dr. Sammie.

"Boyfriend? Is it her? Did you see the photo?" Dr. Sammie asked.

"Yes … I saw the photo, and it's her, but some time ago. Probably seven or eight years ago. Carlos wanted confirmation that Sunshine was not lying to him. The truth is … she's not lying to him. She saw the photo and simply does not remember," Dr. Sanchez shared. "I confirmed it, but I told Carlos that he should have her psychologist examine her and try to help her recall the men in the photo. I told him that psychiatry was not in my realm of practice."

"You told him what?" Dr. Sammie asked, shaking his head.

"The psychologist is to be you," Dr. Sanchez said.

"Me?" Dr. Sammie asked.

"Yes. You can go there, pretending to be her psychologist, and maybe somehow convince him to release her back to you. Carlos is not a stupid man, but if you do convince him that she needs hospitalization to get his answers, then maybe you can get her out of there. It's a long shot."

Dr. Sammie became silent. His thoughts were racing. *The photo must be of Winston and his brother. What they told me was true,* he thought.

"How do you know he'll agree to allow me to do an evaluation?" Dr. Sammie asked.

"Because he trusts me," Dr. Sanchez said. "Carlota will call tomorrow with his instructions for your visitation."

Dr. Sammie stared at Dr. Sanchez. *Is he telling me the truth?* he thought. *Do I trust him?*

"There's no other way, other than going in with guns. And if that happens, Sunshine will be the first one killed," Dr. Sanchez said matter-of-factly.

The brief moment of silence was broken when Dr. Sammie confessed, "I'm pretty sure I know who the men are in the photo."

Dr. Sanchez gasped, "What? How would you know that?"

"It's a long story, but I found out today that one of the owners of that big resort is Sunshine's boyfriend. He was with her the night she fell off the boat into the water," Dr. Sammie shared.

"For a fact?" Dr. Sanchez asked.

"Yes," Dr. Sammie replied.

"Then, that's your answer. When you go in as her doctor, you can suggest that you can help him find the men. That's the leverage you need to get her out of there," Dr. Sanchez said.

"I hope I haven't told you too much here," Dr. Sammie said, questioning his sharing the information with Dr. Sanchez.

"No. I know nothing here," Dr. Sanchez said. "I want to help, but I know nothing…"

Suddenly the conversation was interrupted with a ding from Dr. Sanchez's cell phone. He looked at the text message.

"I gotta go. The hospital is calling me. Looks like there was a bar fight between two men and both are needing medical attention," Dr. Sanchez said as he stood. "I'll call you as soon as I hear from Carlota, which will probably be sometime tomorrow."

Dr. Sammie stood and said, "Okay. I'll be waiting for you call."

Dr. Sanchez extended his hand for a handshake. Dr. Sammie hesitated, and then he shook his hand.

Chapter 16

Sammie tossed and turned all night, trying to get a good night's sleep. He rolled over and looked at the clock, and it displayed 6:26 a.m. *A good time to get up and start my day,* Sammie thought.

Sammie showered and was getting dressed when he glanced at the wound on his shoulder. He moved his arm around and up and down, and even though it was stiff and sore, he decided not to wear the sling. *I think it's time to get rid of this,* he thought. *I hope it's healed enough for some action.*

Sammie had just finished eating his breakfast and was sipping on his second cup of coffee when he heard his cell phone ring. It was Dr. Sanchez.

"Good morning," Sammie said.

"Good morning to you. Did you sleep well last night?" Dr. Sanchez asked.

"Nope. Too much on my mind," Sammie replied.

"I'm sure," Dr. Sanchez said and changed the conversation. "I just heard from Carlota. Carlos wants to meet you…midnight tonight…on his yacht, which will be anchored out of the cove out in the ocean."

Sammie took a deep breath and said, "That's a set-up. You know that…to meet out in the ocean, and at midnight. I'm being set up here."

"Not by me," Dr. Sanchez said quickly. "I agree with you, but I had to let you know this. Tell me that you won't go…or can't go…and I'll call Carlota and tell her that you're out of town. I'll tell her whatever you want me to say. But you told me to tell you everything and keep you informed. So, I am. Carlos wants to meet you on his yacht, and you are to examine Sunshine tonight at midnight. But you do not have to go."

There was a moment of silence. *What should I do?* Sammie thought. *It may be my only chance to rescue Sunshine. Is Dr. Sanchez setting me up?*

Sammie broke the silence and asked, "Will you be going with me?"

"No. I won't be with you," Dr. Sanchez replied cautiously.

There was another moment of silence.

"Tell Carlota I'll be there," Sammie said.

"Are you sure? You're on your own here," Dr. Sanchez said.

"I have a plan," Sammie said.

"Sammie, I'm sorry that all this has happened. And I wish I could be with you. I'm worried for your safety. You can't take any guns with you, and you'll be alone. Are you absolutely sure about this?" Dr. Sanchez asked again.

"Yes. I understand. This is an opportunity to get Sunshine out of there. If I don't go, she'll end up in the ocean…again…and this time, she'll be dead. And if I do go, we both may end up floating in the ocean. I've got to go. Confirm it," Sammie said and ended the phone call.

Sammie immediately made another phone call.

"Hello. This is Lisa," Lisa answered.

"Lisa, this is Dr. Sammie. I need to see Winston, ASAP. It's urgent," Sammie said.

"Okay," Lisa said slowly. "But Winston isn't on the property right now. He'll be back this morning around 11 o'clock."

"I'll be there," Dr. Sammie said.

"Is everything okay?" Lisa asked urgently. "Is Jan okay?"

Sammie didn't answer her and ended the call.

* * *

Sammie pulled his boat into the resort's harbor at approximately 11:00 a.m.

He was greeted. "Visiting or will you be staying for a while?"

"I have an appointment, and I'm expected," Sammie said coldly.

"Yes, sir. Is your appointment with Lisa?" the greeter asked.

"No. It's with Winston…your boss," Sammie snapped.

"I'll take to you to the lobby and Lisa will greet you," the greeter sheepishly said. The greeter texted Lisa.

Lisa was waiting in the lobby when Sammie stepped off the cart.

"Thank you," Sammie said to the driver and turned to Lisa.

"What's the rush? You're scaring me," Lisa said.

"Is Winston here?" Sammie asked, ignoring Lisa's question.

"Yes. He's expecting you," Lisa said and pointed for Sammie to join her on the elevator. They never spoke a word to each other as they rode to the top floor.

They arrived on the floor, and Lisa told the receptionist that they were expected. The doors automatically opened.

Sammie and Lisa walked inside, and Winston was sitting at the bar with Buckie and Allison. Henry was working behind the bar.

"I see the family here sticks together," Sammie said sarcastically and sat down on the sofa with no invitation.

"Is this about Jan?" Winston asked hurriedly.

"Yes. I heard from Carlos…indirectly," Sammie said. "And may I have a drink?"

Winston motioned to Henry to prepare a drink for Sammie. "I'll have a gin and tonic," Sammie said.

"You heard from Carlos? What did Carlos want?" Winston asked earnestly. "Is Jan okay?"

"Your cartel boss has agreed to meet with me. He thinks that I am Sunshine's psychologist and wants me to evaluate her mental status to confirm that she has amnesia," Sammie said.

"Okay. When do you meet him?" Winston asked.

"Tonight…at midnight…outside the cove, in the ocean," Sammie said. "I need you to go with me."

Allison gasped, "What?"

"That's a set-up," Buckie interjected. "A set-up to be murdered."

Sammie looked at Winston and said, "I need you to go along with me to drive the boat. I will explain that I don't feel comfortable being out in the boat at night by myself, and—"

Sammie was interrupted by Buckie. "It's a set-up! You can't go," Buckie said loudly. "He's taking you...and us...to the man who's searching for us. You can't trust him. He's going to get us killed. We need to stick to our plan. Not his."

"Shut up!" Winston yelled.

Sammie darted a sour look toward Buckie and said, "Your plan? Exactly what is your plan? Sitting here doing nothing?"

"I can explain later," Winston said. "And this does seem to be a smoother plan anyway."

"I'm not a part of this, and you shouldn't be either, Winston," Buckie said. "This is all too convenient. All this is...is a way to get us killed. And Jan is probably already dead."

"Sunshine is alive. I don't care if you believe me or not. I'm not asking *you* to help. You can stay here and stay safe. That's what cowards do," Sammie said.

"He's no coward," Allison said rudely. "And we don't know you."

"But I know you...all of you. You allowed a woman, who all of you claim to love, to remain in the ocean to die and...and now...she's in harm's way, again, and you don't want to do a damn—"

Sammie was interrupted by Lisa, "Let's all calm down. Just calm down. We can work together here. We have to."

"All of you...out!" Winston said loudly. He looked at Henry and said, "You too."

No one moved.

"I said, out!" Winston yelled.

Henry almost jumped from behind the bar to the side door exit.

Lisa exchanged a look with Allison, and Allison exchanged a look with Buckie. They all walked out of the room, slamming the door behind them.

"Now. Tell me what you have in mind," Winston said.

"I'm to meet Carlos at the break of the cove out in the ocean. I need you to drive the boat. I'm sure we won't be able to miss his yacht. We'll deal with his reaction to the two of us when we get there. We can't take guns or cell phones. They'll be tossed away. But I will take my medical bag. We need a fast boat, because my troller won't be fast enough if we need to make a quick getaway. I'll be back here at 11 o'clock and we'll leave from here. Are you up for this?" Sammie said.

"Yes," Winston said without hesitation. "Meet me down at the dock at 10:45, and I'll have a boat ready…But what is the plan?"

"The plan is to get there … and see how it plays out. Will you be recognized by him? You mentioned earlier that he wouldn't recognize you, but are you sure?" Sammie asked.

"I had plastic surgery, so I don't think he'll recognize me," Winston said. "How was this meeting set up? Who contacted you?"

"A fellow doctor, Dr. Sanchez, has a half-sister who works for Carlos. She is the go-between. She called Dr. Sanchez, and he called me," Sammie explained.

"So, is that how Dr. Sanchez is involved?" Winston asked.

"Yes. Carlos arranged for Dr. Sanchez to evaluate Sunshine, and Dr. Sanchez suggested that her psychologist see her. And I'm the psychologist," Sammie explained. "He wants limited involvement here because of his family. He knows that Carlos is a dangerous man."

"Do you trust Dr. Sanchez?" Winston asked.

"Yes, I do," Sammie confirmed. "I know that it seems like a set-up, but I don't believe that it is. Dr. Sanchez saw Sunshine. He talked with her. He told me that she was doing okay under the circumstances. But Dr. Sanchez told me he didn't trust Carlos. Dr. Sanchez feels the same as I do. We think that if Carlos finds no purpose in keeping Sunshine, he'll kill her. If she can't provide the information he wants, he'll have no reason to keep her around. And that's where it gets a little tricky. You'll have to follow my lead and let me convince him that she needs medical care. You can't go haywire when you see her. You have to remain calm...indifferent. You can't let on that you know her. And you cannot expect Sunshine to recognize you. In fact, it may be best that she doesn't; that's another risk."

"The whole idea is risky," Winston admitted. "But this is the best chance we have to get Jan out of there."

"What was your plan?" Sammie asked.

"I was trying to convince Buckie that we should meet with Carlos and give back his money. I was thinking of inviting him here as a guest, and meeting with him," Winston shared.

"Buckie agreed to this?" Sammie asked.

"No, not yet," Winston confessed.

"And you were going to do this without telling me?" Sammie asked.

"You stormed out of here from our last meeting. I wasn't sure how to handle it. But I guess we don't have to figure that out now, do we?" Winston said.

"So, you're okay with going along with my plan?" Sammie asked.

"Absolutely," Winston said. "And Buckie should be in another boat out in the ocean, spying on us as an extra precaution."

"If he'll agree to do that," Sammie said, "he can't be seen. He'll have to stay out of sight. But from what I have seen here, Buckie is thinking of his own skin. His attitude needs to change."

"I'll talk to him," Winston said.

* * *

The night's sky was dark and ominous with clouds dancing over the stars. It was close to 10:45 p.m. when Sammie pulled his boat into the harbor at the resort. Sammie turned off the engine, grabbed his medical bag, and stepped onto the dock. The dockmaster greeted him and pointed to Winston in a boat at the end of the dock. "Sir, you're expected."

Sammie saw an idling jetboat with beaming navigational lights at the end of the dock.

Winston motioned for Sammie to get onboard. Sammie stepped onboard, looked around, and asked, "Is this your boat?"

"Yes. I use it for offshore fishing sometimes, but tonight it's on a mission," Winston said and pulled out of the harbor.

Chapter 17

The ride from the resort to outside of the cove into the ocean waters was an easy 25 to 30 minutes. The waves were calm until the boat entered into the ocean. Waves were white capped and suggesting bad weather not far away.

"There's a storm brewing," Sammie said.

"Yes. I know. I saw it on radar. There's a possibility that we'll not take a direct hit," Winston said.

Sammie grabbed the nighttime binoculars and scanned the ocean. "There. I see it. Take a look," Sammie said and handed the binoculars to Winston.

Winston looked and saw what appeared to be a large vessel. "Yeah, I think so. It's lit up like a Christmas tree and looks like a small cruise ship," Winston said.

"I don't think that's a cruise ship," Sammie said, taking back the binoculars. "How far out would you say?"

"About another 10 minutes or so," Winston said and put on a baseball cap.

As their boat got closer to the lit-up vessel, it was clear that it was a super yacht.

"I think this is it," Sammie said in low voice. "I'm in control here. Do you understand?"

"I understand. And by the way, Buckie is watching," Winston said. "But at a safe distance."

Sammie nodded.

As Winston pulled their boat to the back or stern of the yacht, Sammie yelled, "Ahoy. Permission to board."

Two heavily armed bodyguards pointed their rifles at Winston and Sammie. Winson cut off the engine, allowing the boat to drift. Winston raised his arms slowly in the air.

Sammie waved his medical bag in the air. "Permission to board. I'm the doctor."

One of the bodyguards pulled out his walkie talkie and said something in Spanish. The other bodyguard grabbed the line and secured the boat.

"Did you understand what he just said?" Sammie asked in a whisper.

"I think he said something like the doctor is here but not alone," Winston replied quietly.

Both Sammie and Winston stood as if they were statues. They didn't move.

On the other end of the walkie talkie, Carlos asked, "What do you mean…there are two?"

"Si," the bodyguard replied.

"Okay. Check them, and escort them onboard," Carlos said.

"Carlota," Carlos yelled, "were you told that there would be two men?"

Carlota walked up the stairs from the downstairs bedroom.

"No. I didn't know," Carlota answered.

Sammie and Winston climbed a few steps upon the deck. The two bodyguards escorted them along the deck. One of the bodyguards walked in front of them and the other bodyguard walked behind them with a gun pointed at them. Sammie walked in front of Winston. They walked along the deck, and the leading bodyguard tapped on glass door leading into the saloon, which was a luxurious living room.

As they entered through opened sliding glass door, Sammie scoped the layout. A full bar was to the right of the entrance with four stationary bar stools. The way they entered appeared to be only entrance from the deck. In the front of the bar was a long, contemporary-designed, dark wood dining room table with eight high-back cushioned chairs. The luxurious room was so large that there was a staircase winding up to the next level. Beyond the staircase was the living room that served as an expansive lounge area. There were two elegant beige leather sofas with plush pillows on each side of the room. Four modern barrel-style armchairs with sleek coffee tables were stationed throughout near the windows for the view. There were two loveseats at the end of the room facing inward with a foot stool at each one. The large windows offer panoramic views of the sea and were adorned with remote controlled blinds for instance closure. There were two one-of-a-kind modernly designed floor lamps secured to the floor and positioned at the end of each sofa.

Sammie observed a woman standing at the back of the room, where there were stairs leading to the lower cabins. *That must be Carlota*, he thought.

Winston walked in slowly behind Sammie, and whispered very low, "This is Carlos's resort."

Carlos sat at end of the dining room table facing the starboard side of the yacht. The bodyguard pushed Sammie and Winston farther inside. They stood near the other end of the dining table.

Carlos motioned for one of the bodyguards to leave. The other bodyguard walked over to the port side of the bar and stood near where Carlos was sitting.

"Greetings. But I only expected one to arrive…the doctor. You are the doctor?" Carlos said to Sammie.

"Yes, sir. I am Dr. Drillenger. This is my driver…the captain of my boat. I never make it a practice to be out in the water at night without a captain," Sammie said.

"So…he's your captain?" Carlos said condescendingly. "I only needed you here."

Winston looked down to prevent Carlos from making eye contact. Sammie remained quiet. He observed that lying on the table was a remote and manila folder.

"Okay. You," Carlos pointed at Winston, "you sit down over there." He motioned to Winston to sit in one of the barrel chairs, which was about 12 feet from the dining room table. Winston kept his head lowered, pulled at his baseball cap, walked over the chair, and sat down.

"Dr. Drillenger, do you understand that I have a guest that I wish for you to examine?" Carlos asked.

"Yes, sir. I understand that she is your guest, and she is my patient. She has amnesia as a result of a boating accident," Sammie replied cautiously.

"May I see your medical bag?" Carlos asked.

Sammie handed his medical bag to him. Carlos opened it and took out each item. The items were a stethoscope, a bottle of tablets labeled for anxiety and another bottle labeled ammonia salts, and a small hand towel with sanitary hand wipes, ointment, bandages, and Band-Aids. Carlos placed everything back in the medical bag and handed it back to Sammie.

"Our guest—your patient—needs to provide information to me," Carlos said. He opened up the manila folder and placed two photos on the table.

"You see these photos?" Carlos asked and pointed to the one photo with four people. "In this photo is your patient. Her name is Jan Foster. With her is her boyfriend . . . and her boyfriend's brother . . . and the brother's girlfriend. The brothers owe me money. They stole from me. I want to know where they are. I want what was taken from me."

Sammie looked at the photo. He recognized Jan. He was relieved to see that Winston didn't look too much like the man in the photo. Sammie did recognize Allison.

"You know them?" Carlos asked.

"No, I do not know them," Sammie said and picked up the photo, walked over, and showed it to Winston. "Do you know any of these people here?"

Winston looked at the photo, never making eye contact with Sammie or Carlos. He stared at the photo and shook his head.

Sammie placed the photo back on the table. "When was this taken?" Sammie asked.

"A few years ago, but that is your patient. Her name is Jan Foster," Carlos replied.

"Does she know that is her name?" Sammie asked slowly. "I mean … did you tell her that?"

"Yes. I showed her these photos. She claims that she doesn't know her name. She claims to be called Sunshine. That's not a name," Carlos said. "You are here to get the information from her that I need."

Sammie hesitated and said, "I'll do what I can."

"I hope you understand. You will make her tell me what I want to know," Carlos insisted. "Carlota, bring our guest here." Carlos grabbed the remote from the table and closed all the blinds. He stood up, walked over, and pulled the center dining room chair away from the table, and he turned it around so it would be facing the living room area. He remained standing, watching for Carlota to bring Sunshine into the room.

Sammie stood motionless and continued to hold onto his medical bag.

Carlota walked from the downstairs cabin to the long living room, guiding Sunshine along the way. Winston and Sammie froze in shock when they saw Sunshine. Dressed in jeans and a light sweatshirt, she was barefoot, had a canvas bag over her head, and her hands were zipped behind her back. She was struggling to speak.

Carlos took her arm and pushed her down onto the chair. He removed the bag from her head, and it was clear why she couldn't speak. Her mouth was tied with a handkerchief. Carlos returned to his chair and sat down.

"This is your patient … and my guest," Carlos said snuggly.

The bodyguard snickered. Winston and Sammie were horrified at the sight of Sunshine. They were motionless.

Sunshine looked around the room. She recognized Sammie standing next to her. She looked up at Sammie with big, tear-filled, frightened eyes as if pleading, *Help me.*

Sammie walked over in front of Sunshine and looked down at her. He couldn't believe what he was seeing. She had a black eye, both eyes were almost swollen shut, her face was bruised, and there was a recent cut on her face.

"What the …Is this how you treat your guests?" Sammie yelled, losing control.

The bodyguard raised his gun and pointed it at Sammie. Carlos slowly stood up and pulled his gun from his belt and pointed the gun at the side of Sammie's head.

"You are in my house, and you do not speak to me that way in my house. Do you understand?" Carlos yelled.

Sammie regained his composure. He took a deep breath and breathed out slowly. He stared directly into Sunshine's eyes. He slowly turned to face Carlos and stared deeply into the Carlos's eyes. The gun was now in Sammie's face.

"Do you understand?" Carlos yelled.

Without a warning, Sammie slammed his medical bag into Carlos's head. Carlos lost his balance and dropped his gun. Through a quick, precise karate move, Sammie grabbed Carlos's arm, twisting it and pulling to his back, bringing Carlos in front of him as a shield. At the exact moment, the bodyguard fired shots. Bullets sprayed Carlos's body. Sammie violently pushed Carlos's dying body into the bodyguard, knocking the bodyguard to a stumble. The bodyguard dropped his rifle. Sammie dropped to the floor, grabbed the rifle, and as the bodyguard reached for his side gun, Sammie fired the rifle, killing the bodyguard instantly. He fell onto Carlos's dead body.

Winston ran to Sunshine and pulled her to the floor, and he picked up Carlos's gun that had fallen. They crawled and hunkered down behind the back of a sofa. Carlota was already hiding behind the sofa.

"Is everybody okay?" Sammie asked in a loud whisper.

"Yes," Winston replied in a panicked tone.

"Stay cool. Don't panic. It's not over yet," Sammie instructed. "Don't stand up, and lay flat on the floor. Do it now!"

With one hard jerk, Winston removed the handkerchief from Sunshine's mouth. She tried to speak but Winston motioned for her to keep quiet. Winston struggled to break free the zip ties that had her hands bound.

"I have knife," Carlota whispered. She reached into her pocket, opened the knife, and cut the zip ties off Sunshine's wrists. "So sorry. You no deserve this."

"Do what Sammie said. Lay flat," Winston instructed.

Sammie watched the windows, and even with the blinds closed, Sammie saw the shadow of the second bodyguard walking slowly on the deck. Suddenly, the bodyguard disappeared.

Sammie moved very low to the floor. He searched for a light switch on the wall. He was able to cut off all the lights except for the lamps. He knew that the second bodyguard would try to ease the sliding glass door open and shoot his way into the room. Sammie figured the windows were bulletproof. When the bodyguard's shadow disappeared, Sammie guessed that the bodyguard was crawling slowly to the sliding glass door.

Sammie hunkered down in the dark corner of the room behind the bar and next to the door. The sliding glass door eased open very slowly without a sound. Suddenly, the bodyguard burst through the opening with his gun firing blazing bullets from the left to the right throughout the room. He hit the sofas, the walls, and anything in between.

He stopped. There was no movement. The bodyguard stepped farther inside, puzzled to see no one. He looked around the room. Sammie raised from his crouching position, fired his rifle at the bodyguard, striking him so violently that he dropped his gun, stumbled backward out the glass sliding door onto the deck, and staggered into the railing, falling overboard.

Sammie stood up and let out a sigh of relief. "Carlota, how many souls aboard?" Sammie asked quietly.

"Two bodyguards, me, Carlos, and captain," Carlota answered calculatingly.

"The captain," Sammie said surprised. "Stay behind the sofa."

There was a cold silence.

The moment of silence was broken with the start of a boat engine. "What's that?" Winston asked in a low voice.

Sammie rushed to the door and saw boat lights disappearing into the darkness. He stepped back inside and said, "The captain has abandoned the ship…with our boat. It's all done, Winston."

There was no answer.

"Winston, are you okay?" Sammie asked cautiously.

There was no answer. Sammie cut on the light switch.

"Winston?" Sammie said and walked over to the sofa.

"Mr. Sammie, Winston shot," Carlota said. "Can we come out?"

"Yes, you can come out now," Sammie said and walked over and peered over the back of the sofa.

Winston, dazed, was trying to sit up on the floor.

"Winston, are you okay?" Sammie said as he jumped over the back of the sofa to him.

"Yeah, I think so," Winston said, holding his hand to his head as blood covered his face.

"Let me see," Sammie said. Sammie examined Winston's head wound.

"Yup…You were lucky. Just grazed your head. You'll have a bad headache, but not much more," Sammie said. "And don't let the blood fool you. You're okay."

"Jan. Jan…Is she okay?" Winston asked in a panic when he saw her lying face down on the floor.

"Jan. Jan…Talk to me," Winston yelled and reached for her.

Sammie pushed Winston aside and picked up Jan's lifeless body and forced her to look at him.

"Sunshine, do you hear me?" Sammie asked. "Look at me. Do you hear me?"

Sunshine groaned, rolled her eyes, and shook her head affirmatively.

"I just want to go home," Sunshine said sadly. "I don't understand any of this."

Sammie hugged Sunshine and said, "We'll soon be home. I promise."

Winston smiled, let out a sigh of relief, and said, "She's okay."

Everyone moved from behind the sofa and sat down on the bullet-shredded sofa and chairs.

"Carlota, we need a cell phone. Do you have one?" Sammie asked.

Carlota reached into her pocket and handed the cell phone to Sammie. Sammie handed it to Winston, "Call your brother. He needs to get here ASAP. We need to leave here," Sammie said. "And Carlota, look for bottles of water at the bar."

"Buckie is close," Winston volunteered. "He's been watching us."

"Call him. It'll make me feel better," Sammie said. Carlota handed a bottle of water to Sammie and offered one to Winston and Sunshine.

"Thank you," Sammie said and watched Sunshine's every move.

"Hey, this is Winston. You got to get here ASAP. Are you near?" Winston said in the phone. "Yes, we're okay, but we have a situation. We don't have a boat…Okay." Winston ended the phone call.

He started to hand the cell phone to Carlota, but Sammie grabbed it and tossed it out the door into the ocean.

"No! My phone," Carlota yelled.

"You can be followed and tracked, Carlota. It's best this way," Sammie said.

"Buckie will be here shortly," Winston said and wiped the blood off his face.

"You're still bleeding. I've got bandages in my medical bag," Sammie said. He walked over and got a bandage and ointment.

"Yes. Looks like you need a bandage," Sammie said and placed it on Winston's head wound.

Sunshine was very quiet. She became focused on Winston. She stared at him, and without warning she said, "You...you and I were on a yacht. Was it this yacht? No...it wasn't this one. But you..."

Winston interrupted her, "Yes. We were having dinner. Do you remember that?"

"Be careful," Sammie warned. "Too much too soon."

Sunshine looked at Sammie and said, "You pulled me from the water."

"Yes. You know that," Sammie said. "We talked about that."

Sunshine looked back at Winston while Winston put his hand to head to adjust the bandage. She became hypnotized by the scar on Winson's hand.

"The scar on your hand," Sunshine said. Her thoughts began to spin. "I've seen that before."

"Yes, Jan, you have," Winston said slowly.

"Jan. My name is Jan Foster," Jan said slowly. "It's not Sunshine."

"Sunshine is your nickname," Sammie said assuredly.

"You gave me that name," Jan said. "But I remember...My name is Jan Foster. I know my name."

"Now, try not to recall too much. We've got to get out of here. We're in danger, and just let your thoughts come to you slowly," Sammie instructed.

"I hear a boat. It's got to be Buckie," Winston said and stood up.

"Wait. We don't know for sure it's him," Sammie warned.

Sammie stepped slowly over to the light switch and cut off the lights. He leaned out the door and heard a low, gruff voice say, "Sammie... Sammie, is that you?"

"Buckie?" Sammie asked.

"Yes," Buckie answered. "We gotta go. The storm is coming in."

"We're ready," Sammie said.

"Come on, everyone...Buckie's here," Sammie said.

"I get our things," Carlota said hurriedly. She quickly turned and rushed down the stairs to the lower level, returning with two satchel bags.

"Take your water bottles with you. Don't leave anything that will put us here," Sammie said. "Winston, you help Carlota to the boat, and I will help Jan."

Winston helped Jan to her feet when Sammie walked over and pushed him away. "You help Carlota to the boat," Sammie ordered.

Carlota stood at the door with both satchel bags. Winston walked to the door, took the bags, and they walked slowly on the deck and down the steps to Buckie's boat.

"Who is she? Why is she here?" Buckie raged. "She can't come with us! And what has happened here anyway?"

"Yes. She is coming with us. I'll explain later. There's a storm coming in. We've got to get out of here," Winston said matter-of-factly. Sammie and Jan stepped out onto the deck.

"I know! I'm one the driving the boat," Buckie snapped. "I'm the one..."

Buckie was interrupted by a distressed voice.

"No! No! I can't go...I remember...I was pushed...No, I fell...I fell overboard. I was on a yacht! This yacht...No...not this yacht. Winston was there...He's not Winston. His name is Jackson. I'm confused," Jan rambled and shook with fear.

"Sunshine, look at me," Sammie commanded. "Look at me."

"My name is Jan. I can't go...I can't get back in the water. Don't make me go! No!" Jan yelled.

Sammie grabbed her chin. "Look at me," Sammie said.

Jan tried to pull away. Sammie held tighter. "Look...at...me," Sammie said slowly. "Breathe slowly. We are in danger if we stay on this yacht. I will not allow you to go into the water. But you have to get in this boat. Do you remember who pulled you from the water? Do you trust me?"

Jan didn't answer. "Do...you...trust...me?" Sammie asked again.

"Yes," Jan said slowly.

"Then trust me now. You can remember what happened to you... You can remember falling into the water, but you do not have to relive it. I won't let you," Sammie said. He wrapped his arms around her and pushed her in front of him. He walked her along the starboard deck toward the boat.

"Winston…Winston…Help lift Jan into the boat," Sammie instructed.

"I don't trust him," Jan said, bewildered, stopping to look at Winston.

"I won't hurt you. I promise," Winston said. He extended his hands to her.

"We've got to go!" Buckie said urgently.

Jan shook her head from side to side, "No!"

Sammie lifted Jan up and tossed her in the air to Winston. Winston caught her and wrapped his arms around her as they dropped down in the boat. Carlota grabbed Jan's hand and said, "You okay now."

Jan's thoughts were spinning. She had visions of places, people, and things. It was all jumbled, but when she looked at Winston, her thoughts became centered. Winston pulled her close to him and whispered, "You're safe now." Jan looked at him, confused.

Sammie stepped onto the boat and said, "Wait! I left my medical bag." He jumped out of the boat and rushed back into the saloon on the yacht. As he picked up the bag, he saw the photos on the table. He picked them up and pushed them in the medical bag. He hurried out the door and quickly jumped onto the awaiting boat.

"Let's go," Sammie said.

"Finally," Buckie groaned under his breath.

The approaching storm moved closer with its strong, howling winds. The light rain and the sea salt beat on everyone's faces with blinding force. The white-tipped ocean waves seemed to be gaining strength, becoming higher and more violent. The boat tossed back and forth on the ocean waves. It seemed the waves tried to swallow the boat. Buckie struggled to control the speeding boat through the raging waves.

"Hang on, everybody," Sammie said and moved by Buckie.

"We're almost home," Buckie said confidently. "We'll make it."

Chapter 18

Lisa and Allison patiently waited for everyone to return to Winston's and Buckie's top floor suite.

"Where does Henry keep snacks?" Allison asked and walked behind the bar, placing her cell phone there.

"On the second shelf. Have you heard from Buckie?" Lisa asked.

"Not since you asked 30 minutes ago ... and not since he texted me to let me know that he was headed to the cartel's yacht," Allison said. "That's all I know. Want a snack?"

"Something's gone wrong," Lisa said. "No, I don't want anything to eat. Not sure how you can eat right now."

"I'm nervous," Allison said. "That storm is getting closer and stronger, and they're in that boat or with the cartel. I'm nervous."

* * *

Everyone in the boat was relieved when they saw the lights of the resort. They were out of the ocean's violent waves. Buckie eased the boat to the back of the resort where there was a private enclosed dock. The garage door was open, and he maneuvered the boat inside.

"We all have guardian angels, and they worked overtime tonight," Sammie said, smiling, and jumped out of the boat and assisted Buckie in securing it.

Winston lifted Jan to her feet and helped her onto the small, enclosed dock.

"Where are we?" Jan asked.

"We're..." Winston said when Buckie interrupted.

"We're home, and that's where we're going to stay," Buckie snapped.

The boat was tied down, secured, and Buckie closed the garage door.

"The elevator is straight ahead on the right," Winson said, pointing.

Sammie grabbed the two satchel bags and helped Carlota out of the boat.

"I still don't know why she's here," Buckie said and pushed his way past Sammie and Carlota.

"I'll explain," Winston answered.

Everyone crowded onto the elevator. No one spoke a word.

* * *

Lisa and Allison both jumped when they heard the sound of the elevator. They both ran to the front door, and when Lisa opened it, there stood Winston, Buckie, Sammie, Jan, and Carlota. They were wet, covered in blood, and their hair was matted to their faces. Their clothes were dripping with salt water, clinging to their bodies.

Lisa gasped, "What the hell happened to you all?"

Winston walked in, leading Jan. "Lisa, get towels from the hall closet."

Allison ran to Buckie and hugged him and asked, "Are you okay?"

He kissed her on her forehead and said, "Yes. I've been through hell and back, but I'm okay. Just wet and tried."

Allison turned and looked toward Jan. Allison was shocked at what she saw. Jan's eyes were swollen, and she had a black eye with a cut on her face. Her healing scars were visible. She only had a new growth of hair. *She doesn't look like Jan*, Allison thought.

Jan looked around the room. *I've been here before*, she thought. *I remember, I've been here.*

Allison walked over to Jan, and they stood staring at each other. She reached and touched Jan's face. "Jan, do you remember me?" Allison asked slowly.

Jan nodded. "I think so. Your name is Allison...You're my friend."

Allison smiled and hugged Jan. "I missed you. We're best friends."

Lisa returned with the towels and handed them to everyone. Winston took his towel and quickly wrapped it around Jan.

"You're safe here," Winston said to Jan. "I'll take care of you."

Winston looked at Allison. "Allison, take Jan to the master bedroom. She can shower and sleep there tonight. I'll grab some clothes from my room and sleep in the guest bedroom."

"Jan, are you okay? Do you need anything?" Winston asked.

"I'm sort of confused. But...I remember things...and faces are familiar," Jan said with a slight smile. "But I'm so tired...and thirsty."

"Get her some water and juice and even a snack," Sammie interjected. "She's dehydrated, I'm sure. And that's not good for her recovery."

"Come on. We'll take care of that," Allison said and pointed to Jan to follow her to the master bedroom.

"This belong to her," Carlota said in broken English and handed one of the satchels to Allison.

"Lisa, show Sammie and Carlota to the guest rooms down the hallway. And we'll all plan to see each other in a few hours...around noon for brunch," Winston said.

"Who is she?" Lisa asked abruptly, staring at Carlota.

"She's with us," Winston quickly replied.

"She's my friend," Sammie said.

"Taking in another woman?" Buckie said sarcastically.

"More than you would do," Sammie snapped.

"Come on. Let me show you both to your rooms," Lisa said sweetly, diverting an argument.

"I need a strong drink, and then I'm going to shower and go to bed," Buckie said.

Winston looked Buckie and said, "Good. And wash off that nasty attitude."

Allison led Jan into the oversized master bedroom suite. The room was complete with a small kitchenette, a sitting area with a sofa, and a love seat. The room was decorated in soft pastels and the large sliding glass doors captured the view of the ocean and led to an oversized balcony.

"I've never been in this room," Jan said, looking around the room.

"No. You were never in this room," Allison confirmed. "The shower is to the right. I'll get you some pjs, and I'll be back shortly."

"Thanks," Jan said as Allison walked out of the room.

Jan walked into the bathroom. The bathroom was very large with a full-size jacuzzi and a soaking tub. There were endless views from the floor-to-ceiling windows. Jan stepped over to the windows and for a moment, she watched the raging storm. *I'm lucky to be here. I'm lucky to be alive*, she thought.

* * *

Allison walked into her and Buckie's suite. Buckie sat in the sitting area and was sipping on a drink. "Hey, sweetheart, are you sure you're okay?" Allison asked.

"Yeah. Just trying to relax," Buckie replied.

"I'm going to change into my pajamas and take some pjs to Jan. I think that it's best for me to stay with her tonight," Allison said as she changed clothes.

Buckie didn't reply.

"Jan's really been through it. Did you see her face? Her face looks terrible," Allison continued.

Buckie didn't reply.

Allison walked over to Buckie and said, "You don't think Jan should be here, do you?"

Buckie looked at Allison, then looked away. "I'm glad that she's alive. But she's going to bring the cartel down on us."

"But it's not her fault," Allison said softly. "You do know that what you and Winston did was the reason that Carlos had Jan in the first place. What happened tonight?"

"I don't know, but I believe everyone on that yacht was killed," Buckie said and took a sip of his drink.

"What do you mean, killed?" Allison asked.

"You saw us...Everyone was covered in blood. And that bandage on Winston's head was there because a bullet whisked by him. So, you see, if all on that boat was killed, someone will come after us, for sure."

"Winston said that he would tell us everything later," Allison said. "Maybe if all of them are dead, then...Maybe that's a good thing."

Buckie stood, kissed Allison on the forehead, and said, "Maybe. You go on and stay with Jan tonight. I'll see you in the morning."

Allison smiled and walked out.

* * *

Jan showered and wrapped a towel around her body when she heard Allison enter the room.

"Hey, here's a pair of pjs," Allison said joyfully and laid them down at the bathroom entrance door.

A few moments later, Jan walked out of the bathroom dressed in the pjs. "It was so good to shower. And I'm so tired," Jan said as she got onto the bed.

"Do you want a snack, a drink, or more water?" Allison asked. "I'm sure we can find something here."

"No. I just want to go asleep," Jan said. "That is...if I can go to sleep."

Jan got under the bedcovers and Allison cut off the lights and laid down on the sofa.

There was complete silence when Jan asked, "Allison, did I…Do I…Well…Am I supposed to be in a relationship with Winston? He's Jackson, right?"

Allison hesitated and answered, "You and Winston, who changed his name from Jackson, were very much in love. You adored him…and he adored you. Still does."

"But on the night I fell overboard, what happened?" Jan asked.

"You don't remember?" Allison asked.

"No. Not clearly. And I feel confused when I look at Winston," Jan confessed.

"Jan, you are alive and among the living. You've been given a second chance at life…and love…with Winston," Allison said.

The room was quiet, and only the roar of the storm could be heard when Jan softly said, "Or with Sammie," and her words faded as she fell asleep.

Allison, surprised at her comment, never replied.

Chapter 19

By mid-morning, the rain had stopped, and the clouds were clearing away. The bright sunshine peeked through the scattered clouds. The clouds danced across sky, being pushed by the warm tropical breeze.

Allison awoke around 10:45 a.m. She decided to get up and get dressed for the day. She looked over at Jan, who appeared to be sleeping soundly. Allison tiptoed out the room and slowly closed the door behind her. She walked down the hallway to her and Buckie's suite. When she walked inside, she saw Buckie sitting on the balcony, drinking a cup of coffee.

"Good morning, sweetheart. You're up early," Allison said cheerfully and walked over to the kitchenette and got a cup of coffee.

"I guess," Buckie said. "It's almost 11 o'clock, and I guess we're having brunch at noon."

"Yeah. I'm going to shower and get dressed for brunch," Allison said. "In case you're wondering, Jan slept through the night."

"She's probably the only one who did," Buckie said bitterly.

"Buckie, please try to show that you do care about Jan. You don't wish for her to be dead, do you?" Allison said.

"Of course not. It's just a bad situation . . . for all of us," Buckie said.

* * *

Buckie and Allison walked into the front living room, and Henry has set tables along the wall and was preparing the conference table as a dining table with a white tablecloth, floral arrangements, and silverware.

"Good morning, Henry," Allison said. "Has the brunch been ordered?"

"Good morning, and yes, ma'am. Winston left a note on the bar last night with instructions, and I've already called it in. A full brunch for seven to eight people to be served at 12:30 p.m., which will be in about 10 minutes. Would you like a brunch cocktail?" Henry suggested.

"I think I'll have a mimosa," Allison said and smiled.

"Sounds like a good way to start a brunch," Winston said as he entered. "How's Jan this morning?"

"She was sleeping soundly when I got up. I'll go and check on her," Allison volunteered. "Hold my mimosa."

There was a click, and the doors opened. The waitstaff entered with the food, and Lisa, Sammie, and Carlota were walking behind them.

"Good morning," Lisa said. "I think everyone's on time."

"Yes," Sammie agreed. "Looks like it."

"Great," Winston said. "Set up the food on those tables at the wall."

"Yes, sir," the waiter said.

The food was prepared and set on the tables for a buffet serving. It was a full buffet with pancakes, fruit, bacon, muffins, scrambled eggs, toast, avocados, jellies, and more.

"Maybe I should go check on Jan," Winston said.

"I'll go with you," Sammie quickly said.

They both walked down the hallway and tapped on the door. The door opened.

"We're on our way," Allison said. "Jan is getting dressed."

"Is she feeling okay?" Sammie asked.

Jan walked out of the bathroom and said, "Yes, I'm feeling okay, but I'm hungry."

Winston rushed to her side and said, "Let me walk you to the table."

They entered the living room, and everyone approached the buffet. Buckie was sitting at the bar with a plate of food and already eating.

"Everyone, help yourself to the buffet and Henry can prepare any drink for you. Anything you want, including coffee," Winston said and smiled.

"Coffee sounds good," Carlota said.

"I agree," Jan said.

After getting food, everyone sat down at the dining table except for Buckie.

"Buckie, you can join us here at the table," Winston said.

"I'm good here," Buckie replied.

"Well…I'm ready to hear what happened last night," Lisa said as she took a bite of her food.

"Oh, yes…by all means. Tell us, Winston. What happened last night?" Buckie said condescendingly.

Winston ignored Buckie's remark.

"Henry, I would like my usual drink," Winston said as he sat down with a plate of food.

"I can make the story short," Sammie said. "We went to rescue Jan, and we did."

"But you all were covered in blood," Lisa remarked.

"Because there was someone who got gun happy," Buckie snapped.

"No," Winston said. "It was kill…or be killed. We had no weapons, and when Carlos brought Jan out, she had a canvas cover over her head and her hands zip-tied behind her back. When Carlos removed the bag from her head, she had a handkerchief over her mouth."

Lisa gasped. "What? Jan, I am so sorry. I guess that explains all those bruises."

Jan never answered. She felt numb recalling how frightened she was when Carlos questioned her about the photos.

"When I had the opportunity, I took advantage of it," Sammie said. "I've had military hand to hand combat training. I saw a chance, and I took it. Carlos was going to kill all of us."

"Si…Yes…He would kill you," Carlota interjected.

"So, you played Rambo and killed everyone," Buckie said.

"Buckie, it was no game. We're all in danger," Winston said, "including Jan."

"All on that yacht are dead?" Lisa asked.

"Yes," Winston replied. "There were only two bodyguards, Carlota, and Carlos."

"You killed them all?" Lisa asked.

"Yes," Sammie answered. "Except the captain of the yacht. He made his escape with our boat. And that's why Buckie had to come to our rescue."

"If they're all dead, then who will come after you?" Lisa asked.

"His son," Carlota answered slowly.

The room became very quiet.

Sammie broke the silence and asked, "His son? Carlos has a son?"

"Si," Carlota replied.

"And where is he now?" Winston asked. "He wasn't on the yacht."

"He no like what his dad do. He wanted no part of the business. He and Carlos never get along," Carlota said in broken English.

"That's just great," Buckie said. "Now, we'll have the son after us… all of us."

Sammie ignored Buckie's sarcastic remark and asked, "What's his name?"

"His name is Antonio," Carlota said. "I had picture on phone… You threw phone in ocean."

"Antonio? Are you sure? Antonio González?" Lisa asked slowly. She turned her back to the group, walked over the buffet table, and picked up a glass of mimosa and took a big gulp.

"Si," Carlota said. "He travels a lot. No visit much."

"Where does he live?" Sammie asked.

"He live in U.S., where there is snow," Carlota replied.

"Where there is snow?" Winston asked.

"Si," Carlota said. "He like to play in snow."

"Colorado?" Sammie asked.

"Si. That where he live," Carlota said in broken English.

Lisa walked over to the sofa and sat down.

"Are you okay?" Winston asked Lisa. "You look pale."

"I'm fine," Lisa said. "All this killing is—"

"—going to be killing us," Buckie said, interrupting Lisa. "He'll come looking for us."

"But we didn't really kill his dad. His dad was killed by his own bodyguard," Winston said. "Sammie didn't really kill Carlos. The fatal bullets came from the bodyguard's gun...not one of us."

"Well, doesn't that make everything okay? Did you see the morning newspaper?" Buckie asked bitterly.

"Yes. I saw it," Winston snapped. "The headline reads 'Cartel boss found dead in bloodbath on yacht.'"

"So, the coast guard has already found the yacht? Where's the newspaper?" Sammie asked.

Henry, behind the bar, reached to a lower shelf and handed the newspaper to Sammie.

Sammie scanned the article and said, "There's no way that we can be put at the scene. The article indicates that they retrieved a canvas bag and the scarf used on Jan's head and mouth, but there's nothing to point a finger at any of us. I took the photos and threw Carlos's gun in the ocean. They have nothing to go on. In fact, the article suggests it was a dispute between Carlos and his bodyguard."

"You seem to forget that the captain abandoned ship in Winston's boat," Buckie said harshly. "He not only knows who was there, but he can easily identify us. It'll won't take them long to know who that boat belongs to, and they'll be here seeking revenge, all because we had to go rescue…a dead person."

Suddenly, Jan burst out in tears. She got up from the table and wobbled. She was dizzy and stumbled. Allison quickly jumped up and wrapped her arm around Jan's waist.

"That's enough!" Allison said and gave Buckie a look.

Winson jumped up, and so did Sammie, both reaching for Jan. "No," Jan said. "I just want to be alone."

"Let's get you back to bed…You need to rest, and ignore what everyone is saying," Allison said sweetly. She walked Jan to the bedroom.

"Yes," Lisa chimed in, "as if she's not been through hell and back, and now you tell her that we all in danger. And you insinuate it's all her fault!"

"We are in danger," Buckie said, raising his voice.

Winston turned and walked over to the end bar where Buckie was sitting and grabbed Buckie by his shirt collar. "I love you as my brother, as my business partner, and as a friend, but if you ever throw another nasty slur toward Jan…especially for a situation that you and I created, I will knock the holy…" Winston said and was interpreted.

"Come on. Calm down. You're brothers, and obviously you've been through a lot," Sammie said calmly. "Just calm down."

Winston and Buckie stared at each other. Buckie was frozen with surprise. He was shocked at Winston's outburst. "I…I apologize, brother. It's not Jan's fault," Buckie sheepishly said. "I really didn't mean to be blaming her. I'm sorry. I'm just concerned."

"Well…me too," Winston said, and he let go of Buckie's shirt collar. "We'll figure it out. We always do." The brothers exchange a hug.

"We need to find out about the son—where he lives and what he does—and find out all we can about him," Sammie suggested.

"He not work. He not married. Carlos give him money," Carlota said. "I know this because Carlos's wife, my best friend, told me before she die. She wanted son to get marry, but he not marry."

"When was the last time you saw him?" Lisa asked as she made her way back to the table for another mimosa.

"He visit a few weeks ago. He had girlfriend to go see. He only stay two or three days. He left," Carlota replied.

"Do you know where he was going?" Lisa asked and sat down. It was the second time that Lisa's phone dinged.

"Do you need to answer that?" Winston asked impatiently.

"No...not really. The first time was Todd texting me his flight information. He'll be here tomorrow. And the second message is from my assistant. We have an excursion this evening...a sunset cruise. I guess I should go and make sure that's everything okay with it," Lisa said. "Carlota, do you remember where Antonio was traveling to when he left?"

"No...I do not know," Carlota answered.

"Carlota...your half-brother, Dr. Sanchez, does he know Antonio?" Sammie asked.

"Si. He know him," Carlota answered.

"I'll see what I can find out from him," Sammie said.

"Guess I should run on. But I'm going to check on Jan before I go," Lisa said. She set down the empty mimosa glass, picked up two full glasses, and walked toward the bedroom.

Lisa knocked on the bedroom door. Allison opened the door. "Thank you," she said as she reached for the glasses.

"Where's Jan?" Lisa asked.

"She's in the bathroom. She's changing into her pjs and wants to rest," Allison replied.

"Okay. I just wanted to her to know that we all are very happy that she's alive and back with us...no matter Buckie's attitude," Lisa said.

"I know. Buckie's just worried," Allison said in defense of Buckie.

"I've gotta run," Lisa said. "My assistant has texted me several times. Gotta see what's going on."

"Sure. And thanks for the mimosas. I'll let Jan know," Allison said and winked.

Lisa closed the door behind as she left the room. Jan slowly walked out of the bathroom.

"Here. Lisa brought this to you. She wanted to apologize for Buckie's attitude," Allison said and handed the mimosa to Jan. "And I want to do the same. Buckie is just worried. He really is glad that you are alive and back here."

Jan reached for the mimosa and took a sip. "Are you sure?" Jan asked bitterly. "He acts like he wishes that I had stayed dead."

"No. When Buckie is worried, he seems to attack the wrong people and say the wrong things," Allison explained. "He's glad you're okay . . . just like the rest of us. All of us . . . we were just horrified when we thought that you were dead. And to learn that you were alive and not dead! Jan, we love you," Allison said tearfully.

"I am so confused," Jan confessed. "When I look at Winston, I don't know which emotion is stronger . . . love or hatred. And when I look at Sammie . . . I feel safe and protected. And yet . . . outside of both of them, I have no feelings at all. It's like I have no past, and no future. I am just here."

"Jan, do you remember the times we shared?" Allison asked. "I'm your best friend . . . That was in the past . . . and . . . now . . . in the present. I want you know that you have a friend no matter what. I'm here for you."

"I recall us going shopping, being at the lake . . . and I remember the heartbreak you had when Lambert died. You loved him," Jan said, puzzled.

"Yes, but it was different. I thought Buckie was out of my life, and I went on with my life. You didn't. You never gave up on Jackson, or should I say Winston. And now, we both have a future waiting for us with the men that we have always loved. And they have always loved us. Just let go of the past, Jan. It is holding you back. And your past is dead. You died. What a new beginning! You can choose to do whatever you want to do. You can move forward," Allison said.

"Yes, but I can never go back. Right? Because the past is dead," Jan said sadly.

"But what does the past have to offer you? Your friends, your business acquaintances, your co-workers…all have moved on. To them, you died. And yes…the role you played in their lives has been either eliminated or replaced by someone else. It is the here and now that matters. You are alive. Live for today and tomorrow," Allison said.

"I don't know who I am today. I only know what I was in the past. And I am confused about tomorrow," Jan explained.

"Okay. You loved Winston. And he is here and now, and today, and he promises you tomorrow. That is who you are," Allison said. "You can go back…but what will you have?"

Jan shook head. "I don't know."

"Get some rest. We'll talk again. Anytime you want to talk, I'm here for you. But the most important thing now is for you to completely get well. Rest," Allison said.

"I am exhausted with all this," Jan said and relaxed back onto the bed.

"I'm going to sit out here on the balcony for a while, so if you need anything, I'm just steps away," Allison said. "Okay?"

"Thank you … and thank you for everything," Jan said and closed her eyes.

Allison slowly carried her mimosa out the door to the balcony and walked quietly out. She eased herself onto the long chaise lounge and stared out at the ocean. She took a sip of her mimosa and thought, *What is Jan going to do? What is going to happen if she decides to go back to what she thinks is her home? Her home is here now. How can I convince her of that?*

Allison knew that the life Jan had was gone. Jan's past was as dead and buried as Jan was supposed to be. It was obvious through Jan's nightmare kidnapping that Winston was very much in love with Jan. But it was clear that Buckie was worried about the cartel finding them, and if the son, Antonio, would want revenge for his dad's death. Sammie wanted to help, but he was in the way of Jan and Winston getting back together. Was he a friend or foe? How did Carlota fit into all this?

Allison fell asleep in the lounge chair wondering, *What does the future hold for us?*

About the Author

JAN HOWERY, a native of Southwest Virginia, writes with an Appalachian influence. She has been featured in numerous anthologies, including *Broken Petals, Wild Daisies, Scattered Flowers, Daffodil Dreams, Steamy Creek: A Cozy Romance Anthology,* and the complete *These Haunted Hills: A Collection of Short Stories* series. Other writings include fashion and health columns for the Appalachian regional magazine for women, *Voice Magazine for Women.* Her debut novel, *Gone Before Breakfast,* released in 2023, is the first in Howery's *Whisper Cozy Romance Mystery* series.